THERE LIES
A TALE

THERE LIES
A TALE

ERNEST ELLIS

WILLIAM B. EERDMANS PUBLISHING COMPANY

Grand Rapids, Michigan

The words of Heinrich Himmler were quoted from The Rise and Fall of the Third Reich *by William L. Shirer, p. 966 by permission of Simon and Schuster (New York, 1960).*

The words of Andre Malraux were quoted from his Anti-Memoirs, *pp. 398-99 by permission of Holt, Rinehart and Winston (New York, 1968).*

To Rachel Armoc

"... I also want to talk to you quite frankly on a very grave matter. Among ourselves it should be mentioned quite frankly, and yet we will never speak of it publicly ...."

"I mean ... the extermination of the Jewish race.... Most of you must know what it means when 100 corpses are lying side by side, or 500, or 1,000. To have stuck it out and at the same time—apart from exceptions caused by human weakness—to have remained decent fellows, that is what has made us hard. This is a page of glory in our history which has never been written and is never to be written...."

—Heinrich Himmler
to his SS generals
Posen, Oct. 4, 1943

"The degradation of the camps lay above all in the combination of madness and mockery.... The supreme objective was that the prisoners, in their own eyes, should lose their identity as human beings...."

—Malraux

A PREFATORY REMARK

I was seated, not long ago, on a bench in Central Park, sunning myself after a tiring day on the Street—whoever has had experience on the Street will sympathize, such days being not uncommon, when all of the best information of that day seems to have come from the Devil himself and the scales become heavily weighted against one, and although, in jest, one might blame his ill fortune upon a sin of excess of the night before, he knows it is the Devil—as I say, I was sunning myself, tossing a peanut now and then to a friendly pigeon, minding my own business, contemplating a trip to the zoo on the coming morning (I have a fondness for animals, harboring a yen to free them all, and shall yet) when a young man came along and asked if he might not share my bench.

"Of course," I answered, as I continued feeding the pigeon, which had begun eating from my hand.

That should have ended the matter. I was about to leave. There was a good three feet of bench remaining to my right. The young man, however, stood on my left, casting a long shadow, and in a most matter of fact, if not peremptory tone, asked if I wouldn't move over, that he preferred that portion of the bench on which I was seated.

"Really, my good man, I've been quite courteous in not objecting to your sharing my bench and, indeed, I've taken much less space than I'm used to taking, and I don't see why you insist upon sitting precisely where I'm sitting. We don't live in a jungle, you know. . . . See here, you've frightened the pigeon away."

He smiled most enigmatically, explaining that he hoped to sit where I was sitting because of the sun and the fact that I would cast a shadow to my right, in which case it would make it most difficult to read a manuscript which he was in the midst of proofreading, and since there were a good many errors in punctuation and his eyes were not what they once had been, he having spent many hours during the last several nights completing it, he had hoped to have a good light by which to complete a careful reading.

"Ah, then you're an author!" I responded,

moving quickly to the far right of the bench. (I had a high regard for writers.) "I do beg your pardon about the bench. You may certainly sit where I was sitting."

"I'm really not, by profession," blushed the young man, still smiling as enigmatically as before, holding his manuscript as though its weight was more than he was used to carrying (and yet, it appeared for all that, to be little more than the size of a magazine) "I'm really a stockbroker by trade, or was. . . ." He was still smiling, hesitant about taking the place I had vacated. (On close scrutiny I could see that the smile was a result of a nervous condition, the facial muscles having frozen in a particular position; and on closer scrutiny yet, the smile was hardly a smile at all, hard lines having just begun to form at the corners of the mouth in a downward curve.) "I still am, I suppose, although it's been a long time, I'm afraid I can't say just how long, that I've been away from the office. . . . There was this confession . . . tale, I thought I should get down . . . he spoke almost without stopping for about three days, or maybe it was four . . . and I was afraid that if I tried to tell someone about the jewel without their understanding . . . they thought I was mixed up with

. . . I'm not a jewel thief, I can assure you of that. . . ."

"I don't quite follow you, I'm afraid. Although I, too, play that hazardous game on the Street and was just gathering myself after a rather trying afternoon with Anaconda Copper, and can understand that sometimes the strain of such a day can . . . well, can possibly unnerve one. . . . A scandal, perhaps? Some trickery with numbers? Is your office in the midst of a general house-cleaning? Your house deals in rare jewels, I take it. . . ."

"You don't understand," the young man insisted, taking the place I had vacated on the bench. The enigmatic smile gave way to a grimace, the downward forming lines around the corner of the mouth now accentuated by a twitching that was most unpleasant to look at.

"I was a fool . . . I've never seen! . . . Unbelievable! . . . " he went on, as though I weren't there. "I was an utter fool for calling. Why couldn't I have waited? The old woman! The flower vendor! . . . He didn't believe I had a fiancée and she doesn't believe me . . . philandering, she said!" Then turning to me, his face flushed, as though more angry with me than seeking the pleasure of my company, he asked, almost shouted, "Would you care to have a drink?"

"I'm sorry. I don't usually drink with strangers. I'm afraid I haven't followed you at all. If you'll excuse me then, my wife is having a few people in before dinner."

"Good day to you, and God bless your martini," he retorted, as he tried to control his twitching with a nervous laugh.

"You can get on with your proofreading without any shadow cast from the left," I answered, indignant at his presumption.

"Yes. I can get on with my proofreading. Be off with you, clerk. And may your soul. . . . Hurry, or you'll be late. Your lovey-dovey wife might rap your knuckles for getting your fingers into the strawberry jam."

"As I surmised when you first walked up and drove the pigeon away," I glared back, "you're not a man of business at all, but one of those beat and angry young men who would take every bench in Central Park and paint them red just for the sake of a national scandal. I know your kind. It's what one gets for trying to be courteous to a passing stranger. Yes, I enjoy my martinis and intend to have half a dozen just to wash away the bad taste you've left. You may live in a zoo, if you please. It's your business. But, I'll be back within two hours to sit on this bench as is my habit after dinner each evening."

"As you wish. But don't say I didn't warn you," he retorted scornfully, moving to the middle of the bench. "Should you see a man with thinning hair, hot coals for eyes and a skin tanned with the fires of Hell who gave the name of Rudin and disappeared jewel and all and left me. . . . Never mind. You'd never understand. Be off with you, clerk. . . ."

"When did they let you out?" I shot back from a distance in the Street. "I do intend to return and I trust that I'll be permitted to take up my old place without any further ado."

"By all means. A pleasant good evening to you, Excellency; and please, do convey my best wishes to your fiancée . . . your wife! Yes, and may you have most enlightening conversation over cocktails," he shouted, laughing a sardonic laugh that fairly filed my spine as I turned my back and started up Fifth Avenue, my feathers ruffled.

To think that I moved over and gave him half of my bench so he could proofread without any shadow from the left and he mocked me for it, I thought, gritting my teeth. God bless the French for still having the guillotine. They ought to shave a few writers with it every morning before they sit down to what they call work—you've heard them, each one has his own line about how he starts at seven in the morning, no matter how late he goes to bed, and works steadily until one, at which time he has lunch, then a swim, after which he relaxes by reading the classics in his field; hah! Or another who begins at nine and never allows himself more than two hours of concentrated labor a day, otherwise he goes stale; and the less they work, the more silly women ogle them as though they came from another world and were above the whole shebang—a good close shave every morning with the guillotine would do the trick; they'd come flying down to earth again, I tell you, and not demand the whole bench, wherever they are. So ran my thoughts, and I believe you'll agree, justifiably.

Well, I did. I downed half a dozen martinis straight off at that innocent little affair my wife was having to welcome an old schoolfriend back to the city. I was in my best form, I tell you, even though I was obliged to listen to him, one of those dabblers of the school of the absurd, chattering away about how he writes to please himself, scorning the Old Masters, Heaven and Hell, and all that went before, looking as innocent as a lamb as he was twitting the young ladies with his eyelashes. I felt as though I could take the whole city of New York and slice it in half horizontally and have a look wherever I chose. Sometimes, even the most mediocre of us human beings get that feeling. We become giants, as it were; and if the dull-witted would try to take the romance out of life by saying it was the martinis, we know better. We are, after all, descended from flesh-eating giants who wrestled with dinosaurs, and even if half a million years have elapsed, the traces of the descent are not altogether gone. You've had that feeling, too. You've been sipping a martini, dazzled by a magnificent bust hovering before your eyes; you feel that you could, with your eyes alone, disrobe it. It's a feeling not far removed from that when you feel you could tear the Manhattan phone book in two with your bare hands. Of course, in my case, part of the feeling was anger. The young man on the bench had gotten under my skin. I was determined to return and give him a piece of my mind. I did go back, the party still going strong.

You're right. He was gone. Just as I thought.

He'd taken my bench and hadn't made an hour's use of it. Proofreading, indeed! He was probably rendezvousing with an accomplice.

But wait! A manila envelope, a remarkable self-portrait sketched upon it. There was a rustling in some bushes nearby. Whoever had been there was now gone. I walked several dozen yards in each direction looking for him. I waited until dark. I took it home. No, I didn't open it. I went back the next day and the next, at the same time. I placed an advertisement in the personal columns of all the newspapers over a period of seven years. No response.

I then read it, yes. I took it to a friend who was a friend of a friend who had many friends in the literary world. (I didn't trust the judgment of that long eye-lashed writer of the avant-garde, or any of his friends, to whom my wife insisted I show it for critical appraisal.)

"Absolutely not," I insisted. "They treat everything but their own work with contempt. The first thing you know, they'll want to edit it, add a phrase here and there, jazz it up with some sex, in short, stamp it as their own, and I won't have it. One day the author of it will turn up and then you'll have a libel suit on your hands." That cinched the argument. I seldom win an argument from my wife. Few men really do. They may think they do; in fact, their wives encourage them in believing that they always win their arguments and although it would take an Immanuel Kant to prove such to most men (when one lives in a man's world, he surrounds himself with myths as he embellishes upon those that are centuries old, implanted in the psychology of the race) the truth of the matter, the "inner truth" of it, is that men rarely, if ever, win an argument that is worth winning. But win this one I did. How? By the threat of a long, drawn-out libel suit and the possibility of utter impoverishment. (How quickly the mind responds! All judges can't be bought, no matter whom you know, and one immediately brings to mind a stickler for the law who refuses to adjourn his courtroom after a week of summer temperatures ranging in the high nineties.)

"For goodness sake, do as you like with it then. Why did you have to bother me with it at all? I'm not interested." That's how the argument ended. Ah, you've seen through her reasoning! You've understood how quickly her mind worked! How much better it would be anyway, she thought to herself, if none of her literary friends know of it beforehand.

The manuscript follows then. I only wish it had been possible to reproduce it, as written—the script, I mean, photographed from the original sheets, with several half pages of blank space scattered throughout, as though "the author" had intended to return to them. I say, "the author," even though I suffered such abuse at his hands. He is, however, "the author," having put down, as he heard it, a tale told by another man, as you'll see.

If I may go on here for a sentence or two, let me explain the choice of title, *There Lies A Tale.* The manuscript had been given none, although a clue was found, the word "twice" scribbled on the first page (above the text) as it was again on page forty-three. He may have intended then (the supposition is entirely my own) to call it *A Twice Told Tale.* There was the first teller, of course, and the stockbroker who listened (the one who stole my bench, to whom I've referred as "the author") who transcribed it as he had heard it on each of three or four successive days. (I have, in the forepart of this explanatory preface, transcribed his words as I heard them.) Thus, my deduction about what his choice of title might have been (the word "twice" found twice). He was the second teller. It would naturally have been an act of outright theft, if not dishonesty, to have called it *A Twice Told Tale,* in addition to its being misleading to the reader, who would have, in time, discovered that the story was not really "twice" told, but rather "thrice" told. There was the first teller (in whose words the story is really told) and the stockbroker, who became the second teller, and finally, myself, who, no matter how objective I've been in rendering it as found (there were the blank spaces which I didn't attempt to fill in, which I eliminated simply by running what was writ into the next written passage) would have to be counted the third. I would then have had to rightfully call it *A Thrice Told Tale,* which would have been disconcerting, since one does not readily warm to something being told at third hand. The problem, then, was to give the manuscript a title which made one feel as though he had discovered it and were listening to the first teller himself. Thus, *There Lies A Tale.*

Finally, a word, if I may, directed to the "author" with the hope that he may see this. He will, no doubt, wonder whether I yet bear him a grudge for what I suffered at his hands. Although I did feel it proper to have described my feelings at the time, which I think he will perhaps now agree were not unjustified, No, I do not; as I trust he will approve of my choice of dedication.

He should also know that I have since encountered Rudin, who expressed deep regret about the mistrust and the circumstance under which they parted, for he liked "the author" very much, as a matter of fact, hoped to see him again, his feeling towards him friendly, because he ("the author") had been the first who had really been willing to listen and, of course, the first to see the jewel. He (Rudin) had revealed himself to me only after I had sought out the flower vendor who had known Armoc. "The author" knows, of course, that the old woman was not easily found. He could have made it a good deal simpler by mentioning the address.

Will he consider, then, seeing Rudin again? I am at the very same bench which I offered to share, each day, unless it is raining.

CHAPTER I

Allow me, if I may, to introduce myself. My name is Rudin. Would you care to join me in a nightcap? Fine. Excellent. After all, it is ridiculous to sit and drink alone at such a late hour. People should be friendlier, should they not? They should break down the barriers, as it were. What's that; you say I sound foreign to you? Well, in a manner of speaking, I suppose I am, although I have adopted your ways and have more or less lost my identity.

What would you like? Brandy? That's my drink, too. Oh waiter, two brandies, if you please.

Have I been in New York long? Not too long, although I come here frequently. I am a buyer. What do I buy you ask? Jewels. By trade, I am a jeweler's merchant. I deal in only the rarest of gems, those which few people can afford any longer. No, not because there is less money in the world. Hardly. If anything, there is more. But because few people can afford to wear them publicly and not appear ridiculous. After all, what woman in your country can wear a precious tiara, embellished with diamonds, finished with the most delicate, lacelike handiwork which once belonged to the Queen of Rumania? The world has changed, has it not? To wear such a piece of jewelry requires an appreciative audience. So you see, I am one of those merchants whose market is rapidly disappearing.

You say that my eyes appear strange? I suppose they might. When one has survived, he surely must reflect somewhere in his countenance the strain of survival. You see, to survive was, in a certain sense, something that one had to believe in. One abandons other things for this belief.

Everyone believes in survival? I agree. Some believe in it a little more than others, don't you think? Those who have taught in the modern era that survival, reproduction of the species was the strongest of human urges, may well have been correct. After all, who can refute science? It has taught us so much. Tell me, sir, do you believe in science? Yes, it has done wonders! How can one afford not believing in it? But, I don't think I made myself quite clear. Do you believe that once a scientific finding becomes the property of man, once an idea proven by the cumulative study of generations of brilliant minds penetrates the consciousness of man, that he will begin to live by it?

Let me enlarge on that a bit. In the nineteenth century, a new, yet not altogether new, idea was generated by an isolated scientist who had brought together intuitions about the nature of man and society. But, more than bringing them together, he confirmed them by the most rigorous scientific study. These intuitions saw man as a higher animal that had evolved out of the lower. They brought a totally new kind of thought to bear upon man and the society in which he lived. Naturally, wars raged in the academies over this revolutionary idea, but it prevailed, so to speak; it became dominant. It began to take on a life of its own and to shape every idea which was from that moment on expressed. Religion, for fear of losing its grip entirely upon its flocks, accommodated itself to it.

You look perplexed. I'm sorry, sir. I should not have presumed to bother you with such abstruse thought. Perhaps it seems irrelevant to matters at hand. I suppose you would prefer to hear about jewels. Indeed, are they not something which man's highest imagination has wrought from crude stone? It requires the hand of man to become a jewel. Take any precious stone found in the bowels of the earth. Before it enters the world, it must first be culled by the practiced eye which has been trained over centuries. It is a knowledge which is beyond science. It actually refutes science, does it not? The chemist can take a stone and analyze it into its component parts. He can break it down into its organic qualities. It becomes zero. But the practiced eye, that which is effected out of the imagination, takes that same stone and conceives a precious whole. His is a master craft that grew out of man's desire to BE. You ask me what I mean by his desire to BE? It's quite simple. Man desired to BE within himself, did he not? There came a point, I do not know quite when, I suppose from the time that man was, to excel, to shine, to BE. He found his image within himself. The highest expression might be, at one moment, to have power over other men, but never power by itself. There had to be that final touch . . . the jewel. What would a mistress be without a beautiful necklace made of precious stone to adorn her lovely neck and bosom? What would the highest order of the church be without a crown composed of jewels? Have not men risked their lives over and over to purloin out of museums some rare piece of jewelry which they could never wear? Indeed, which no one could ever wear. But ah, sir, that is just the point I was making. Some man will pay millions for such jewels, he will purchase a mansion in some far away place, adorn certain rooms with rich tapestries . . . all leading to an inner chamber which represents the ultimate in human taste and there, in the quiet of an evening, alone, quite alone, he will bring from some deep wall safe, placed there by his own hand, these jewels. They will make their way to a desk perhaps, or even better, a pedestal draped in purple satin with hidden lights playing directly upon it . . . and there a sublime moment comes into being, a communication as it were, so delicate, so fine as to have required centuries of seeking. There takes place a moment which literally vibrates with hidden meaning. Man's desire to BE has brought this moment into being. Millions of wills transcending time in that search for the ultimate in being have wrought, as though by magic, this single moment of beauty. This man of wealth surely is not looking at this for himself alone. He embodies those millions of wills that have sought and been denied. If this were not so, we should have to call him quite selfish or insane. How else, sir, could the jewel have such meaning? If I were to take you to my quarters and show you a jewel that men had murdered in order to possess, do you think you would experience that sublimity that our connoisseur knew? You do? Ah, you amaze me, sir. I did not realize that a chance acquaintance would be so fortunate for me. Then we shall, indeed, make a visit to my quarters although I must confess it would be a long walk for both of us. Perhaps another night. Shall we have another brandy? You would like to pay? At your pleasure. I thank you. You are most kind.

Perhaps, tomorrow for lunch? Polo, you said. Oh, yes, tomorrow is Sunday and there is a polo match. You should go, by all means. It is a magnificent sport and I would not care to stand in the way. You say you would rather chat? Not at all. I would not think of it. One must not miss his polo match. Afterwards then? Fine! I shall meet you here at five.

CHAPTER II

Ah, my friend. You are prompt. By my watch, you are three minutes early. Whether you realized it or not, you did not introduce yourself last night. I'm afraid I talked too much, did I not? . . . A wonderful name. And how was the polo match? Excellent. I'm happy that you enjoyed it so much. A young lady you'd like me to meet? Your fiancée? I think I'd like to, but, perhaps, some other time. You say you told her about meeting me last night? How very generous of you. If you don't mind, sir, I don't think I'd like to meet her yet. I don't feel quite up to it. Perhaps we should have our walk first, then another time I might invite you and your young lady to see the jewel we talked about. I'm sure her taste is as fine as yours.

I appear tired, worn? My eyes? They show undue strain? Oh well, as I said last evening, one would perhaps show the strain of survival. Do you like flowers? Come let me purchase one for your buttonhole. This fine old lady will appreciate it. A red rose for you? Here you are. It sets you off magnificently. I shall take a white one. How much, my dear? Here you are, and keep the change, and may God bless you, too. You're very welcome.

People can be friendly in this city when one does such a small thing if one happens to come along at the proper moment. Sometimes I wish I had been a vendor of flowers, that and nothing more. Have you ever strolled through the flower district in this city at the break of dawn? Such activity! A hundred varieties gathered in boxes along the sidewalks waiting to be delivered to their vendors. A flower sets life off, gives it color. Imagine how dull one's existence in this city of concrete would be without them! We are on Sixth Avenue, are we not? Take a look at any one of these dismal apartments and you will invariably see an earthen pot containing some delicate flower, placed on a sill to get the fleeting sun. One does not ask much. To settle for flowers . . . what more should one want? Ah, yes, you ask again about that jewel. It is priceless, sir. But before one can esteem its quality, one must appreciate a single flower growing on a run-down sill.

Why was it so difficult to survive? One would have to go back, oh, so far back. Who knows how far? One would have to study certain moments: one in which an overseer might have whipped a peasant, or another when one man fornicated with another's wife, or possibly when some carriage belonging to a Duke might have run down some innocent wayfarer; or another moment in time when a brilliant young student walked by a cathedral door on a Sunday morning and refused to enter because he wanted to BE within himself.

Life is born, and as it is born, it must die. But before it dies, it must BECOME. There is the will to BECOME. Did not that ninteenth century gentleman gather intuitions together and speak of survival? He who was fit survived. Ah, I am oversimplifying? Perhaps. There comes a moment, however, in each man's life when he desires to BE. It is this moment, that is the product of all his other moments, when he, in fact, plays GOD, and it is at this moment that he has exercised the will to survive. This puzzles you? You say it is not necessarily man's wish to play God?

Fifth Avenue. It is pleasant to stroll along it of a Sunday evening. You live on Fifth Avenue? Indeed. Across from the Park? Wonderful. Let's walk in that direction. I can walk you to your door

Ah, yes, Warsaw. You wish me to continue. I believe I wander, sir, because I do not know quite where to begin. I hardly know if there is a beginning. Perhaps that's what my eyes meant when you said they looked strange.

I shall begin with the occupation. Which? The first of course. I should have said war. But then war is something one forgets. War, in a sense, is clean. One is on one side or another. He does not decide these things. He fights, kills, suffers and forgets. We should begin after the war. I was then, as now, a jeweler's merchant. I had a wife and a daughter. And I, well, sir, I do not know quite how to put it. Let us say that I was dissatisfied. I was driven by some kind of inner lust that had command over me. Shall we say here that I was not aware that it was wrong? Again, perhaps, it was the need to BE. To BE, yes. Inside oneself. There were clients. What did one do? One had always as clients women of leisure. They did not come to my salon. Not at all. They would call. They wished to see rare pieces of jewelry in their homes.

There was one. She played the piano exquisitely. She was a student of Chopin. To play Chopin well . . . that is an accomplishment. How few know him as he should be played. Are you fond of music? Excellent. I hope you like Chopin. Music does something for one if he really loves it.

It moves him to great moments. The man who cloistered himself with his rare gems certainly must have loved music. Wouldn't you agree?

But to get on. I should first tell you what it was like, the occupation. The war was short. They called it the six-week war. We were first. It was like a game of chess on the continent. Each of us waited. Of course there were those who deceived themselves and others. There was the gentleman with the umbrella who had the answer. But then, I suppose that the peasant who was whipped by his overseer had an answer, too, as much as the young man who walked by the cathedral. You see, one could protest. One could even be righteous. One could be anything he chose until the bombs began to fall. One could even keep his nose clean, as it were. Certainly, if one were a jeweler's merchant, he could study jewelry. One could sell jewels to the young woman who played Chopin so well. If one played loudly enough, one could almost drown out the outer sounds.

Warsaw was a busy city. There were demonstrations. There were parades. There were those who spoke of the new science and those who spoke of the barbarians. And then there were those who kept their noses clean. To keep one's nose clean—

ah, sir, that was perhaps the most difficult thing to do. Certainly, one cannot help but be drawn to the crowd, can one now, especially in times that are fraught with the coming event? But, then, one could pass them by. Unless, of course, he was of the ancient race. Man must find someone in all ages for his hatred. How else? As man loves, he, too, must hate. Or, should we say that as he hates, he too, must love? Or better yet, one might even say that hate is but one manifestation of the need for love. There are many answers. Perhaps, it depended upon where one was situated. If one were on a farm in North Dakota, there were the prairies and the sod that was so plentiful.

Let's say you were walking down a Warsaw street and you came to a busy corner and were waiting for a cab, and there was a street meeting taking place right there before your eyes. You usually didn't pay much attention to street meetings. But some young fellow was haranguing in a husky voice. One could feel a nervous twitching in the crowd. And, when one of the ancients came walking down that same street, he suddenly fell. It just happened. He was tripped, you might say, but after all, when there is a street meeting and many people, how would one know whether someone's foot or his shoestring caused him to fall? In less than a twinkling of an eye, he had been kicked and was on his feet, pushed into the street with his outer coat torn.

It does depend, does it not, upon where one is at the moment? I was there. Perhaps I should have helped him to his feet, or at least brushed his coat? But I am, after all, a jeweler's merchant. Yet, the fact that I did not help him to his feet or brush his coat is not what counted. *I hated that man.* Only for that infinitesimal fraction of a second that it fleeted across my mind. Yes. There was the catch. I hated him for that one single fleeting fraction.

After so long, my friend, after so long a time as this, I can still see the dirt on the side of this ancient's trousers. I did not look at his face. Only the trousers. Even the jeers that followed him into the street are no longer there. Only the dirt, at less than an arm's length. Oh yes, I remember the shoes. What thick soles they had! High shoes that any *pauvre* might wear.

Ah, you started to quote those lines:

About suffering they were never wrong,
The Old Masters: how well they understood
Its human position; how it takes place

While someone else is eating or opening a
window or just walking dully along.

Yes, indeed. How well they understood!

We're nearing the Park. Shall we wander into
it a bit before dusk? Do you enjoy ducks? Or do
you prefer to watch the children sailing their
boats? Myself? I enjoy them both. I love to see the
skyline of this city of concrete. A testament to
man's genius. They are brave ones who work aloft.
Are you capable of it, my friend? Walking some
swaying girder a thousand feet above? One says it
is nothing when one is used to it. The pity of it is
that the man who goes aloft does take it for
granted. He does not know that he is a master
builder out of an ancient craft. Each man should
have his own title. He should be king of himself.
The one who walks the girder is a king and does
not know it. But then, perhaps, he, too, is waiting
to share in that moment when the rare jewels are
taken out of the wall safe to be looked at in a
castle.

I wander again? I'm sorry. Let's take this
bench and sit. My soles are thin. My feet tire easily.
Would you care for a cigarette? You've given them
up, you say? Yes, it is a habit. You prefer your

pipe? Lung cancer? Yes, I am aware that there are recent discoveries. But then, one must always die, must he not? That is our one absolute.

To get back. There was the war. War is war. They bombed with live bombs. You have seen newsreels, sir, have you not, taken from one of our winged chariots, of those tiny puffs of smoke dotting a city? It's so impersonal. Bombs away! A moment later, puffs of smoke. And then, of course, there is the pilot seeking his target, wondering whether he actually struck home. Ah, sir, home. Did the man strike home? He surely must have thought of home, one way or another. But, as the saying goes, war is war. We were dismembered. Do not think for a moment that we did not resist. Perhaps I should not have said "we." For there were patriots who died in the streets. But one is too easy with language, is he not?

It reminds me of a poet of Spain. I do not follow such matters, but one day a volume of his poetry fell into my hands. It was not the poetry as such that struck me or made an indelible impression. It was the flyleaf of the book which told about how he died before a firing squad on a hot day in August in Granada, after being dragged through the streets. What should one say to this?

"Dragged through the streets!" Here was a poet. There was a war. The war may have been clean in a sense. But, a poet dragged through the streets and shot before a firing squad? And, of course, there were patriots. Each side has its patriots and each who has survived has reminisced and said "we". The man who stood in an arched window above the square and watched could talk as years went by of the civil war. But one man touched the arm of the poet, hustled him along the street, raised the blindfold to his eyes and turned his back. What was lost, forgotten, spent, was that moment. That one single moment that would have to be communicated another way if it could be communicated at all. It is not that a man died before a firing squad that troubled me. It was the moment that the one turned his back after the blindfold, and walked to his place beside the squad. Count the steps. There were perhaps ten. How long does it take a man to take those steps? You see, the poet must have known how to die. But there was that final single shred of time when one man had to turn his back. There was this estrangement. One had to play God.

At any rate, sir, there was a fierce resistance to the enemy. As I was a jeweler's merchant, I surely could not conduct business as I wished. To walk in the streets was dangerous. However, we had put away a store of food. Our larder was full, as the saying goes. Our home for some reason or other had been spared a direct hit.

Somehow, one even breathed easier when we surrendered. After all, war is war. If one side loses, it is over. Better to get it over with quickly than to go on indefinitely. One has a tendency to trust his enemy. It was, as always, stated repeatedly in messages to the people that there would be no reprisals if the resistance ceased. Law and order would once again prevail. What could make more sense than that? Why should these resisters in the street jeopardize law and order? There had been propaganda. A great deal of it. What should one have believed? Was the enemy as bad as we were told? We had seen the little man on newsreels so often with his moustache and his guttural oratory. He had harangued for hours on end and everyone seemed to believe. There was something mystifying about the millions of wills that seemed to follow. One had seen gigantic gatherings in central squares in Hanseatic cities with torchlights and parades and women fainting and men marching to drumlike beats. What does one say? One had heard people say that, after all, he can not be so bad if so many people are willing to follow. Who knows? And then, one does not, so to speak, wish to presume to know. Lies had been told before.

The resistance ceased. One might say that our youth had come to their senses. After all, one must know when he is defeated, must he not? Can one make the decision to go on claiming innocent lives, bringing forth a much greater disaster, when he knows that the enemy has so much greater resources and firepower?

Yet, even for one who had kept his nose clean, as it were, who had remained aloof, there seemed to be in the atmosphere about one a tension that one could not put his finger on. It might have been one's imagination. Who can truthfully say? There were vague rumors that residents were being hustled off in the middle of the night and being shot for their participation in the resistance. Can one believe rumors? How does such a rumor begin? Does it begin from fact or fancy? How could one know for sure who was a jeweler's merchant.

It was no more than a few weeks after the war had ceased that my valet brought a card into the drawing room from the young lady who played Chopin so well. She had requested the pleasure of my company at dinner that evening. I had not been out of the house for a week. I had been going over accounts, so to speak. I had gone through my whole clientele and erased certain names. I had dropped their cards, as it were, and had been careful enough to throw them into the fireplace. One could not be too sure. What kind of people were these whom I had served as an arbiter of taste? Did their families have a history? One's name did count for something in such times, and of course one had to, in a sense, prove that he had not done business with certain people in the past. So, it was quite simple. One merely removed their cards from his file. He dropped them, and that made an end of it. People disappeared from one's mind. One had his instincts. One did not have to speak or think about such matters. One had only to accommodate himself.

I accepted the dinner engagement quite readily. It was a relief, sir. This was one of those fair signs for which we look so desperately. After the storm clouds, there is always that tiny patch of clear sky that seems to emerge. Well, one might say that this was one of those tiny patches. The storm could not last forever.

For the occasion, I dressed. What a pleasure it

was. One must desire to dress for it to hold such rare pleasure. This desire, I must admit, I had. Call it what you like, a weakness in such troubled times, or what you will. Yet, when one is dressed, let us say that a portion of his manliness returns to him. He BECOMES again. To place one's cuff links in place; to have one's coat brushed. To be perfectly honest, I looked forward to this evening with anticipation.

When I arrived at my friend's country villa, situated most ideally on the banks of the Vistula in one of our most elegant suburbs, need I tell you what a peaceful moment it was, walking the graveled path from the drive to the door? How can one describe it? Here we were, in the very middle of a war so to speak. We were the country on which the eyes of the world were, for the moment, focused. And, here, in a quiet suburb, there was a peace and a majestic calm that was sublime. Shall I call it sublime? You see, I cannot help but remember it well, that single moment, walking on the gravel path. One might say here that one listened to the sound of his footsteps, or to the beating of his heart. The truth, sir, is that one recognized the fact that he had survived. Why had not one of those tiny puffs of smoke struck his home? Or, one might even ask why had he not been one of the patriots who had stood in the street. He could very easily say in all of the confusion that he had, alas, been ill at home with influenza and thus could not venture outside his door. Or, one might have said that his doctor had given him strict orders not to leave his house because he had a weak heart. Or one could say more unequivocally, could one not, that it was fate?

But to get on. When I was ushered into my hostess's drawing room you can imagine my surprise in finding, among others whom I knew, two high ranking officers of our conqueror's airforce. A strange tingling began to take place inside myself. How should one describe it? There they were. Such well-groomed uniforms. Immaculate. One was leaning upon the grand piano talking to a young chap who was a painter. The other was standing in a corner surrounded by two or three gentlemen and ladies, laughing at some joke or other. My hostess took my arm and led me first to one, and then to the other. I can remember well the eyes of the first, who was the younger of the two. How deeply blue they were. There was a warmness in them. They smiled so graciously at me. How could one not smile in return? The other was a more serious chap, yet, courteous, to say the least. After our introduction, I can remember him turning to the young painter and chatting on about Renoir. He had never been to Paris and had been in hopes of one day visiting there. He admired the French impressionists so much.

Tell me, my young friend. What does one do when he is confronted with such a situation? Here were two young men, certainly not at all older than yourself, intelligent, of apparently good family, chatting just as you and I. But they were my country's conquerors, were they not? There were these rumors of young men of the resistance being sought after dark. One could not help but wonder. Yet, there, in my presence, were two most charming young men. How could one believe such rumors about people like this? You should have heard the youngest speak so eloquently about Marcel Proust. Can a vulgar man speak eloquently and with feeling about Marcel Proust? I hardly think so. Yet, while he was speaking about Proust, I wanted to ask him if he had watched the puffs of smoke from his winged chariot. I restrained myself. I enjoyed the conversation immensely. Perhaps that will shock you more than anything . . . not that I was polite, but that I enjoyed the conversation so much. Even though I insisted that I wished to ask him this question, I was enthralled. I controlled myself, to be sure. We must have had several drinks when our hostess played some Chopin for us, and I believe, more perfectly than she had ever played him before.

It does, perhaps, seem strange, does it not, that less than a few weeks after the occupation, this young lady was entertaining two young airmen. You must understand. This was not an ordinary young lady. She had that kind of beauty which only those most famous European courtesans have had. She was widely traveled and as widely read. She had friends in every country of Europe. She was fluent in half a dozen languages. Men of high station would sacrifice their reputations to lay their heads upon her lap. How many had come to myself to purchase some rare jewel for this woman!

So you see, in a sense, perhaps, she was a person who did not have to follow all of the rules. National boundaries had little meaning for her. Obviously, if she were entertaining these two young airmen, what could one say? Perhaps it was the thing to do. Perhaps it was better to be on friendly terms. Who should decide such a matter?

Of course, again, I suppose one might say that it depended upon where one were situated. I was there, my good man. You, I believe, of a younger generation, might still have been crawling upon some floor in swaddling clothes.

After the party had broken up, this fine young lady, as she always had, reminded me of those finest mysteries of the flesh. Do not misunderstand me, sir. Do not for a moment think that she gave her favors freely to anyone who might chance to come along. Far from it. Somehow, we understood one another. Let us put it another way, let us say that I understood her, or better yet, appreciated her. We would sip brandy until a late hour. She would play Chopin for me as I requested. She would allow me to adorn her with diamonds and rubies.

Life continued apace. I did not venture from my quarters except to conduct business or attend some function where my presence as a connoisseur was required. My wife had taken up work in a hospital nearby as a nurse. My daughter continued to teach in school. Rumors flew. Some, perhaps, wilder than others. My daughter told me how our own people had beaten one of the ancients in the street in front of her school. He lived on the border of the ghetto. You see, everyone, in a sense, wanted to keep his nose clean. One could always say that he had never traded with an ancient. This was the instinct for survival again. At any rate, as you are aware, sir, there was a ghetto. Not everyone of this ancient race lived within this ghetto. There were a few who were immune, who could, as it were, live without. But they were few. They, you see, were not pure. They had a confused ancestry. One could not place them properly.

One evening, not long after the occupation had begun, I was sitting in my library studying some gem which I had recently purchased, making doubly sure that it had no flaw.

Outside my study door which led into the garden, I heard strange sounds in the darkness, as though one were listening to a bird with a broken wing uttering its anguished cry as it tried to fly from danger. There were muffled groans that were blurred by the sounds of scuffling feet.

I walked stealthily to a window and peered through the blinds to make out the forms of two husky men in uniform wrestling with a young woman. She was turning and twisting violently, and as I watched, one of these men struck her a lusty blow on the side of the head.

Now, my young friend, let me confess something to you. You have listened patiently until this
moment. Perhaps you will not wish to continue
our walk.

You see, I sensed, nay knew, that this young
woman was about to be ravished. I was alone in the
house. Our servants were out. My wife was at the
hospital; my daughter at a special school meeting.

I knew that the brute force that seemed to be
seeping into our lives was about to pluck its prey.
There had been rumors. And, in addition, I had a
gun. Yes. One did risk his life to possess one. There
had been orders issued for all firearms to be turned
in at our city hall. I had kept mine. I do not know
why. Nothing prepossessing, to be sure. A tiny
pocket pistol. I had but to reach into the drawer
and I could place my hand upon it. I was an
excellent shot.

It would have been an act of magnificent
defiance, would it not? Imagine. Has not our whole
culture taught from ancient days of gallant men of
the roundtable having killed dragons to save some
lovely damsel in distress?

But here is something else again. As quickly as
that moment of defiance had spent itself, a moment which was an eternity in which smothered

sobs were dumbed with heavy hands, another took its place. As I had hated that ancient who had tripped on that busy street corner, *I hated this woman.* Yes, cher ami. The human mind is capable of caprices, is it not? It is like a carousel. It is up to the man at the wheel to stop it at a certain point. How easy it was! This young woman had to be of the ancient race! I could say to myself that she should have been at home with her family. One should remain with his family in troubled times. To venture on the streets when there were these rumors!

You are perspiring, my friend? Have I offended you? I thought as much. Let us then part company. You prefer to continue? *Bien.* It is a pleasant evening.

I listened to the abductors walk briskly away. I did not venture outside my door to bid the young woman enter. To have placed my arm about her shoulder and to have dried her tears! That would have been such an easy thing to do, would it not, monsieur? To have dried her tears! Do not misunderstand me. Do not believe that as soon as my hatred had disappeared, that I did not pity her. Do not for another moment believe that I did not feel an inward rage as I listened to her sobbing quietly.

I knew both pity and rage. I found myself grinding my teeth and cursing. But, alas, it was too late. They had gone. The young lady was on her feet, hurrying towards the street.

Needless to say, I could no longer study my precious gems that evening. I was overwrought. The experience had been too much for me. Something inside myself had given just a little. As you are so fond of saying here, something snapped. I could hear it as clearly as that final plucked string in Chekhov's *Cherry Orchard.* Into one's life there comes an experience. . . . Of course, one might have been in Saskatchewan. But I was not. I was in Warsaw, in my library, studying a precious gem, carrying out my profession, as it were. Were we not speaking a moment ago about fate? People are faced with such circumstances. They are helpless, so to speak. The street on which I lived in one of the more fashionable residential sections of our city was long. There were dozens of spacious gardens; indeed, many of them far more secluded. Why did this have to happen in my garden, outside my library door? A silly question you say? Not at all.

Ah, I should have reached into my drawer and found my pistol? You forget, cher ami, that there was no one in audience. I was alone in the house. There was not a soul in the street. You say that it did not matter; it was a matter of honour? I thought as much. One must not wear his heart upon his shirtsleeve. The church? There is a cathedral close by? I should find some priest and confess my sin? Ah, I see. I do not blame you at all. You are correct. It is painful, yes.

Shall we part company then? I leave it to you, monsieur. I am here at this bench each day at noon. You would like to see the precious jewel? As you wish. Bon soir, and give my most humble apologies to your fiancée for having kept you beyond your appointed time.

CHAPTER III

Ah, my friend. You did come after all. The exchange was not as busy as you anticipated. I took your advice and walked into that cathedral you mentioned. I lit a candle and said a Hail Mary three times. I sought the priest who was in confessional attire. There were several waiting. I did not wish to chance missing you here at noon. I'm glad you came. Be my guest for lunch. I know an excellent Hungarian restaurant on Sixth Avenue. Do you like borscht? Wonderful! Let's walk in that direction.

Two years had passed. The rumors were still there. One heard of strange things in the ghetto. It had been closed off, surrounded, you might say. Like so many others, I had put it quite out of my mind. One accommodates himself, so to speak. A matter of the mind, don't you think? One ceases to think about something and it ceases to exist. You must be aware of that remarkable argument that took place in the nineteenth century between a certain German philosopher and his pupil, whose name has been such anathema to your world— unless one chose to recognize it with his mind, reality certainly could not exist. The other said that reality does for a certainty exist, and its existence is what creates the mind. Who shall say? Speaking for myself, and I suppose for a few others, the ghetto had ceased to exist. I refused to be disturbed. Had I seen for myself? I had not. There were those ugly rumors, of course. But life is full of rumors, is it not? Each moment that we are alive, a new rumor is born.

It was not long before my peace of mind was again disturbed. One evening I went into my daughter's bedroom to borrow a necklace I had given her before the war. I wanted to make a duplicate of it for a very special client. One should not venture into another's bedroom unless invited, but she was, after all, my daughter.

Her jewelry box was kept in the uppermost drawer of her chest. She placed little store upon them. Inside the box, folded over several times, was a sheet of onion thin newspaper. My curiosity was aroused.

When I had it partially opened, I could read three words in bold print:

"Citizens of Warsaw"

As I had begun to read, our front door bell rang. My fingers were scorched! The rumors then were true. Here in my own home, in my daughter's jewel box, was this very newspaper the authorities had been talking about. Whoever possessed or knew the whereabouts of such a document and did not report it was subject to death before a firing squad. This sheet of onion thin paper seemed to have the tenacity that an ordinary piece of newsprint could not have. How shall I say it? It was glued to my fingers. It was as though by discovering it, I had invited disaster. The ring at the door was persistent. Ah, my friend. There had been whispers of the knock on the door. I had a sense of terrible fear compounded of hatred. Not for my daughter, to be sure, but for those who had encouraged her, led her on, so to speak; those who had actually printed the paper. I recovered myself sufficiently to place the document in a wall safe and composed myself enough to scurry to the door.

There was a stranger on my doorstep, an elderly man I knew to be of the ancient race. Disaster! It comes all at once. As you are so fond of saying here, when it rains, it pours.

I had gone through my card file so carefully. I

had dropped anyone whom I had suspected. Yet, here, to call on me, was one of those who had been confined to the ghetto. Then they were not all imprisoned as the rumors implied. There had been lies, indeed.

I bade him enter and asked him his business. He reached into an inner pocket and produced a gem, shaped more perfectly than any I had ever seen. It was red, ruby red. It sparkled with an inner life. I knew that I was gazing upon a jewel more priceless than any I had ever before beheld; that kind of jewel for which man craved in his insatiable thirst for that final power. Great emperors of ancient epochs had traversed distant oceans to seek it for their domain. They had gathered together great armies and marched across the sands of time to search for it. Do not ask me how I knew this. Mine was an ancient craft, as old as man, and I did not bear the title, jeweler's merchant, for nought.

I urged him to state his business. His tale was of a daughter. There was an opportunity to buy her way out of the ghetto to a new home across the sea. There were ways, it seemed. How did one go about it? He would not tell. He had had to choose. Of two children, only one could go. Did his eyes reflect something of this choice? They did.

If there was money, and there was a way for one, one simply chose. Who would go? I asked him whether one stayed awake for nights on end to decide? Or did some unseen hand intrude? I realize, cher ami, that this must be painful. One cannot slur over such matters. There was a choice. As I listened to this old man's tale . . . indeed. I called him old just then. As I reflect, he could not have been over forty. But oh, how old he looked that night! Imagine it, dear friend, he was selling this most precious gem to save his daughter whom he had selected out of two. He, too, in a sense, had played God, had he not? And now it was my turn. With my eyepiece, I studied his possession. I had the choice of haggling over price or understanding at once his mission.

It is at such a moment that one has vision of man upon this earth wending his way. One sees human graves piled to the sky. One sees emperors eating grapes and drinking wine. One hears the laughter of a child outside the door of a peasant hovel. One knows that while he is asked to decide a child's fate, two lovers are holding hands on the plains of North Dakota. And one knows, too, in the innermost recesses of his heart that the rumors, those vague rumors about vans of people being driven into the countryside, have truth in them. He knows that there are trees growing along the road upon which they drive, and it perplexes him. He imagines himself riding in such a van and he looks down at his boots which have mud upon them, then across at his neighbor's boots and wonders if he is living in a world of fancy or reality, and all at once it dawns upon him and he almost smiles inside himself. It is a fleeting smile that tells him it must be fancy. Such things did not and could not in reality happen. When the van stops, they will all alight and go to clean quarters and be given jobs. How foolish it would be for anyone to deliberately destroy people when they could be of use in the world. It didn't make sense. Why did one have boots on his feet? To walk with, of course. Why did one have hands? To work with, of course. Why did one have eyes? To see with, naturally. Why did one have a brain? To think with. . . . Right next to me was a professor of languages. He could teach Aleph, Ba. He could teach sounds, words. People would know how to communicate with one another when he finished. What difference did it make where one originated; he would break down those barriers. And, when the guard came up to him, he would be the interpreter. He would say; we did not believe the rumors and we know that they are not true. There are forty of us here. Shall I give you their names and tell you what each can do? That will simplify everything for you. There, across from me, is a woman who can sing like a lark in three languages. Perhaps you have some soldiers you would like entertained? And, there, see that little fellow? He is a juggler. Perhaps you have a circus in which he can perform? Here on my left is a woodcarver. Perhaps you have some caskets you would like built? Here, standing next to me is a stonecutter. He can carve beautifully. Perhaps you have some gravestones you would like done?

Ah, cher ami, the human mind. It is capable of tricks. Here I was asked by an old man to help save his daughter and I could almost tell myself that somehow we were dreaming.

We haggled. A jeweler's merchant has to haggle. If he paid the price that was asked, he would not be true to his trade. But before long, we had struck a bargain. I purchased the jewel. He departed as quickly as he had come.

Did you enjoy your borscht? Excellent. I'm so glad you did. A cigar? Have one of mine. Choice Havanas. Let me light it for you. You ask about the jewel? It is the one I told you about, the one that men would murder to possess. It's in my quarters. Yes, indeed, I shall show it to you. I'm glad you have a taste for the finer things. Life would be dull, would it not, without such desires.

The underground, you ask? My daughter? Forgive me. I have hesitated to speak about my daughter. I do not know, in truth, whether I possess that right. As her father, I doubt very much that I really knew her. Oh, of course, most fathers will say that they know their daughters as well as they know themselves. But then, one should be modest, in all fairness.

She would not tell me where she had received the newspaper. I stormed, sir, as any father would, and demanded to know precisely what connection she had with this movement against authority. Had there not been enough bloodshed? Did she want more people to go before the firing squad? All of the rumors could not be true about the vans at night. I was sure that they were exaggerated. I had met men in uniform at social functions and they were gentlemen.

She was adamant. She accused me of being unpatriotic, of not caring for my country, that I could consort with the enemy as though nothing had happened.

This pained me. Need I say more? This was my own daughter. My own flesh and blood. Had I brought on the war? Tell me, good sir. I am a peaceful man. I hate war. I plied my trade in all good conscience. When one is a jeweler's merchant, one must be neutral. Jewels transcend national boundaries. I had in my possession, at that very moment, rare treasures that had been owned by Chinese emperors, Indian maharajahs, Austrian archdukes, English princesses, Brazilian coffee merchants. I had served the highest of European royalty. I had created headpieces for coronations. There had been no ball or social function in recent times at which my creations were not worn. One did not have a practiced eye for nought. My craft, sir, was an ancient one, as old as man.

If men wished to fight, then let them fight. Had I sat in on those conferences which determined the fate of millions? Had I participated in those ugly demonstrations that had drowned out quiet evenings of Chopin? I had not. Had I been one of those who was an arbiter of man's fate in trying times, I would have reached into an inner pocket and produced some priceless gem that would have brought affairs of the world back to normal. Come, gentlemen, at ease. I have within the confines of an inner pocket a diamond so rare, so exquisite, that worldly affairs can bide their time. Here, gentlemen, each of you has a practised eye. You are selected to guide and rule. Let's pause a moment and study this stone of antiquity I have placed on the table before you. Let's wonder at its magnificence. Let's recapture that afternoon when it adorned the breast of an Egyptian queen as she walked majestically into a crowded ballroom awaiting the entry of a noble Caesar. It was this very piece, gentlemen, that set her off, as it were. It was the crowning touch. It gave the occasion greater transcendence than any man had known before. In that crowded ballroom were warriors and ladies of noble clans who had reached that height to which man aspires; they stood within the presence of a moment that was sublime. It represented man's yearning for the ultimate.

Yes, cher ami, this is what I would have done. I would have brought silly men back to their senses for a moment. Imagine how simple everything would have been. We could have had an auction. One would wager national treasures to possess such a monument to man's ultimate desire to BE. I would have had warfare confined to some ante-chamber in Geneva and life could have gone on.

You see, I had rare gems that could have kept these gentlemen occupied for months and years.

I jest, you say? Of course, I jest. Why should I not? I have survived, my friend. I am here smoking a rare Havana in an East side Hungarian restaurant.

What was important, however, to the situation at hand, was my daughter. I could easily have appealed to her pity by saying, here I am an old man in a dry month selling jewels, or I could have pleaded a weak heart, or any one of a number of things. But, ah, sir, how does one appeal to youth? Indeed. It may sound simple to you. There was a war. There was an enemy. There were strange things happening in the dark of the night. One could close his eyes. One could even philosophically refuse to accept what he did not see with his own eyes. It was a difficult situation, to say the least. I pleaded, as any good father would do. Did I not say to you earlier how wonderful it would have been to have spent one's life as a flower vendor? Yes, I could have plucked a rose and offered it as a token of my esteem for my daughter's worth. But this, sir, was a most trying situation.

CHAPTER IV

And so began that period in which events piled themselves one on top of the other. One could no longer keep track of all that happened. There was a war on two fronts. Young men were inducted to fight on both of them. The airmen I had met were replaced by others. My friend who played Chopin so well would take mysterious trips which might last for as long as a month. The rumors continued to mount by the thousands. One no longer heard of vans alone. There were chambers that one heard whispers about; chimneys that reached as tall as skyscrapers which emitted strange and peculiar odors.

It was at about this time that I noticed one evening, on my return from another part of the city, a man standing in the shadows near our home; short, spare, dressed with an outer trenchcoat and a dark, narrow-brimmed hat, evidently waiting for some passerby. For how long he remained, or for how many nights he had been in this place, I did not know, and paid it little attention. But one evening at my friend's home, there was a stranger present, a man who didn't seem at home in company that enjoyed good music. Sallow complected, narrow grey eyes, straight hair that was thinning, he approached me during the course of the evening and began chatting. I can assure you I had never met the man, yet there was something quite familiar about him, and it dawned upon me that in shape and form, he fitted the stranger whom I had discovered in the shadows. Despite the fact that I had not seen his face, or come closer than twenty feet to him, I knew that this was the same person. Ah, then, monsieur, the rumor that one had heard of the secret police, whose name had sent shudders vibrating through the whole of the countryside, had had some truth in it. One does not immediately, in such a situation, have all of his composure, especially if he had seen in his daughter's jewel box that onion thin paper which was the organ of the resistance. Instead of one's thinking about music or about art, or about the state of the war, one thinks of the newspaper. If this stranger said good evening quite casually, I must have responded to him as casually, while I desired to tell him right off that the paper was only onion thin and surely such a cheap piece of paper could not be taken so seriously. After all, one little sheet of onion thin paper might also have contained a very businesslike letter, or even a simple memorandum of trade. Why should one assume that it was anything else? Plainly, it was a memo that had come from the superintendent of schools and had read at the top, "Teachers of Warsaw."

And, as our conversation proceeded, in the midst of a thought which I was expressing about Beethoven, a flash came into this gentleman's eyes—a quick flash—and one might not have noticed it if he had not said almost in a whisper, "Did you know, sir, that your daughter is in serious trouble?"

There it was! What one had waited for all along as he chattered on and drank champagne. Have you ever walked in the country on a pleasant afternoon and heard a crash of thunder unexpectedly from some heavy cloud that had seemingly come from nowhere? You have? Then, my friend, you surely can remember how it startled you? So be it. Here was the face of that man-made instrument that had given children nightmares speaking to myself about my only child. I stammered back something which must have been quite silly, such as, "Oh, my, has she fallen out with her superintendent again?"

Our friend smiled. Yes, mind you, he smiled. Such a serious matter as a falling out with her school superintendent, and he smiled. I knew then that I had become frantic unnecessarily. There had been no cause for alarm. It was those ghastly rumors that had unnerved everyone. Why, there I was in a room full of the most cosmopolitan people drinking champagne and listening to my hostess play the piano. She was magnificent.

"There is a newspaper that is being printed. It is undermining civil and military authority. We have reason to believe, sir, that your daughter is part of this movement. Knowing that you are a friend of our hostess, we did not wish to do anything which might be unreasonable. Sometimes fathers can make their children see right from wrong. We would like you to talk to her, monsieur, and see if you cannot convince her to tell you where this paper is being printed. That's all we wish to know. I shall call on you one week from this coming Wednesday at eight o'clock. Good evening."

The gentleman had disappeared. I believe I must have stood nodding to his smiling face after he was gone. My mind must have drifted back into some dreamlike state. I remembered a picnic on the banks of Lake Geneva in Switzerland. It was a Sunday afternoon. One war had just ended. There was an air of peace in this little country. Wounded soldiers were convalescing here and there. There was talk that this had been the war to end all wars. I remembered a boat on the lake which seemed to glide without any effort, carrying some man and his beloved. That's all there was, the lake, the boat, wounded soldiers, my family. Somehow time had stopped, as it often does, or so it seemed, at any rate. Is that not the way, my friend, when something shatters about you. You go back to a moment that is spent and you can almost believe that someone is trying to play a rude joke upon you. You absolutely refuse to believe that there is anything to it.

My hostess aroused me from the blissful reminiscence by kissing me gently upon the cheek. She pouted and said I had paid little attention to her the whole evening and accused me of dreaming about some Parisienne dancer doing the can-can. I reassured her that I could never think of anyone but her.

I hurried home and woke my daughter. In a whisper, I told her what had been said to me that evening. In a whisper, mind you, in my own home.

I felt the presence of that shadowy figure standing on the veranda outside her bedroom window. I pleaded with her to reassure me that the sheet of onion thin paper I had found was nothing more than a memo from her school superintendent. She smiled. Imagine, my friend, at such a moment, one's smiling. She told me outright that it was the organ of the underground and that it was read by everyone in Warsaw. The occupation authorities would never find out where it was printed, no matter how many they arrested, or how many they tortured. She enumerated the crimes they had committed in the name of law and order. She told of how thousands of people were incarcerated in camps and how others were disappearing without trace for no offense whatsoever but for belonging to the ancient race. I was overwrought. I told her that these were bald exaggerations, and she had no way of knowing for sure that these things were being done. Why should people be done away with simply because they belonged to the ancient race, unless, of course, they were resisting?

At these protestations, my daughter wept. She asked how an intelligent man could refuse to believe that such things were happening. One had only to look about him and he could see. Her own school was in the process of being closed. Already more than half of her students had disappeared, either to the army or to a camp.

I used every argument, sir. I told her that war was war, and what could one expect if people resisted. Authority had to be maintained. At least, if there was a resistance to this authority, why did they have to involve young women. There surely were enough men. . . . But that was not it at all. That was not what I had wanted to say. There was authority. There had to be some kind of authority, even during war. To undermine it was to prolong the war, to waste our youth who would be needed for better things when it had ended.

It was at this juncture that the color nearly left my daughter's face. It happened quickly. She no longer looked directly at me. Her eyes were fastened to her bedcovers. Something I had said had moved her to a feeling of shame. I thought that at last I had begun to penetrate that wall of misunderstanding. I began to press her to tell me where the onion thin paper had been printed. At last I felt that this secret would be revealed and we could finish with that sinister figure that hovered in the shadows. Were we talking, my dear friend, of how most fathers thought they knew their daughters? Alas, one surely should not presume what he is unequal to. I had idle visions of our returning to the banks of Lake Geneva. We would be finished with this ugly business. I had clients, after all, in every important capital of the world. I could very easily arrange a business excursion.

Then, to interrupt these idle visions, as though with deliberate intent to thwart her father, my daughter turned towards me with a stare of withering contempt and scorn . . . My daughter, sir, whom I had held upon my knee and fondled. I was her father. . . . The look . . . the look, sir. It spoke an unbridgeable chasm. . . . If I had heard the snap of Chekhov's string at another time, this time I could sense mountains disintegrating at my feet. . . . Was it hatred? I do not know. Call it what you will. She did not speak. I asked her what I had said that had unnerved her. She could not, would not respond. She stared. I pleaded that if she could not tell me what I had to know that at least she might travel to Lodz to remain with her aunt until the war had ended; she surely would be able to teach there; that her remaining there would at least guarantee her safety; to become more deeply involved would mean nothing less than falling into the hands of that sinister figure.

I spent the next seven days pleading with my wife to intervene, to bring our daughter to her senses. She refused. She remained neutral, as it were. She told me of many things she had seen at the hospital; of caring for people whom one could guess had had abusive treatment of one kind or another, people who had been called in for questioning and then released. One did not speak of such matters; one simply understood. If one could not find marks on the body, one nonetheless knew that if a person vomited blood, and he showed no signs of ulcers, he might have suffered internal injuries. Perhaps, he had fallen in the street beneath the wheels of a passing truck.

Somehow our daughter understood that these conversations between my wife and myself were taking place. How did one hide such matters in one's own household? And, although I had not mentioned the exact night that the slightly balding gentleman was to call, both my wife and my daughter knew and it was on that morning, wanting to attempt a final appeal to her good senses, that I went into her bedroom early to find that the room was unoccupied; in fact, that it had not been slept in. . . .

Needless to say, I became quite frantic. I

awakened my wife and told her what had happened. She told me to gain control of myself, to be calm. She had known all along. In my own house, sir, strange things had been taking place behind my back. Secrets were being exchanged of which I had not the slightest notion. I stormed at my wife, told her that she had, indeed, gone too far, that I was still the man of the house, and that to have plotted behind my back was shameless. Did she know what it meant for our daughter to be wandering about homelessly in the streets of Warsaw, sleeping at the homes of strangers, hiding by day and not daring to venture out except at night? And what was I expected to answer to the balding gentleman when he came to call that evening?

My wife had little to say to me except that one had to do what one had to do. There was no other answer at such a time. She trusted the good sense of our daughter. Hard as it was, perhaps she was doing the correct thing. As far as the balding gentleman was concerned, there was little one could say to him. Regardless of what one said, it would be misconstrued. It was better to say nothing at all.

Simple? That sounded simple enough on the

face of it. Merely say nothing at all. When he came to the door that evening, refuse to greet him. When he asked whether I had been able to reason with my daughter, again, remain utterly silent. That was easy enough, as one sat discussing the situation with his wife at breakfast, but as the day wore on, the smiling countenance of the balding gentleman began to hover before my eyes. The smile would turn into a frown. His eyebrows were thin. There are differences in frowns, are there not, sir? If one sees those bushy, unruly eyebrows, which show their frown quite plainly, one does not wonder whether the face is frowning. But, those thin eyebrows that belong to those expressionless faces! They do not show their frown so readily. One looks from the eyebrows into the eyes. In the eyes there is a glitter like the surface of a steel blade. One knows that he is dealing with a cold anger that is impersonal. It is one's business to be angry, so one is angry. There resides behind that anger a strange quality . . . one discerns it . . the impersonal coldness of a power that seeps into one's life. The eyes assure you that it is not you at all at which they are looking, but something beyond you, outside of you, away from you, something out of the past that has become the present and which, even though no longer visible to yourself, is certainly so to the eyes.

I prepared myself as best I could. I dressed. I laid out my best jewels and studied them as casually as I might have any other evening of my life. Inwardly, as the appointed hour approached, I was anything but calm.

Would you care to walk, sir? Did you enjoy your cigar? They have a fine flavor, do they not? An after dinner stroll is most pleasant. Come, let's be off. Ah, the afternoon sun is warm. Tell me, my friend, is there another city in the world with the movement and color of your own on a weekday afternoon? Your captains of industry, men whose domains stretch to the four corners of the globe, mingle and rub shoulders with Cybeles of the earth who ply their trade from bar to bar. Truckdrivers, delivering their wares on one of your cross streets, can make a visiting prince tap his knee in a taxicab while an affair of state waits upon his arrival. Your elevated trains, creeping up like thunder, drown into silence the short, quick curse of a policeman and the poignant cry of a would-be poet, carving his empire from some dingy abode facing the girdered track. Were I not a jeweler's merchant and were I asked where in this world I should like to be deposited to finish out my days, I would say Manhattan.

You would like me to continue, you say? You ask what I said to the balding gentleman who was to call at eight? Nothing. Nothing at all. He did not come at his appointed hour or any other hour, neither that evening or those that were to follow. Every knock, every sound in the evening outside our door increased my anxiety the more. And, as time went on, I knew that they knew that my daughter was no longer there. They had known from the moment she had left our home.

I spent the next weeks wandering the streets of the city, believing I might find some trace of her whereabouts. In the meagerly supplied market stalls or in a half-empty cafe, every face I saw expressed in a silent way, an anguish or a turmoil that remained unspoken. In almost every pair of eyes there was written a tragedy that would remain untold; the tragedy of having known the siren's wail, the hobnailed boot, the puffs of smoke, or the tortured cry of men and women being herded into vans. A deep pain was communicated from one to another. If one closed his eyes for a moment as he sat in a cafe, he sensed about him a terror that seemed to hover like a storm cloud on a still summer afternoon, hidden by a shield of unruffled grey, yet sensed, known; about to burst with all the fury of the elements. One could close his eyes, sir, and know that somewhere behind him, or in front, or perhaps, beside him, there was a life that on the morrow would simply disappear, disintegrate, or explode. If an urchin of the street came up to shine one's shoes, one could read in his eyes a thousand tales of violence—seen, unspoken, etched forever in the deepest recesses of convoluted matter. The whip and bite of the ragged cloth across the shoe were the inanimate outcries of what had become a day by day existence—shapeless, formless, haphazard.

And, after the searching, there were weeks and months of life slipping by, of long days with hours spent in curious thought that could not bring together all of the loose ends of life about me. One can often live on the fringe of something with thoughts that will not take final shape and which as one looks back, seem to have come from a mind other than his own. If one tried to reason, he ended up with absolutes of unreason. One heard of the colored glass in the Cathedral of Chartres having been removed during the war and replaced by ordinary windows. One could muse over this for hours on end and ask himself with what the children of God outside the Cathedral were being replaced? Of course, there was a simple answer for such a paradox; another child could come from the womb in nine months of time; a work of art such as the glass at Chartres represented centuries of man's achievement. As you can see, sir, I am not a philosopher and perhaps do not understand as quickly as I should. Each time I saw Chartres, I had to measure the value of the painted glass by that decision which that ancient had had to make in selecting which of his children should live, and somehow these loose ends of thought all led back to the ghetto and to the child who would remain behind, knowing that he would remain behind, and forgiving in his child's mind his father who had chosen, and from that forgiveness, looking upon a sister with that kind of love which would lead one back to the face of Christ in the painted glass of Chartres.

Forgive me, cher ami. I fear I obtrude a quite personal opinion upon you, and I should not take that license. Thank you; you are most tolerant and kind. Ah, across the street there. A gathering of attractive women, leaving the quiet of a well-made drawing room.

In the room, the women come and go,
Talking of . . . strawberry jam.

I'm sorry. "Of Michelangelo." A terrible slip of the tongue. Sometimes my mind wanders without my quite realizing it at the moment. His line is a fine one. It's what you might call clean poetry. It is crisp. You feel, on hearing it, almost as though you could bite into it . . . or, as I believe you say here, get your teeth into it. Does it not ring with wonderful charm?

How did my thought end upon strawberry jam, when a moment before I had been speaking of Chartres? I really can't say, unless, as I saw those attractive women leaving that brownstone, I was reminded of a young mother standing in line, holding her daughter's hand, in a . . . well . . . they were, as I say, standing in line. The young girl could not have been more than ten or eleven. Somehow, the two of them flitted across my mind's eye, just as I had encountered them, and whenever they appear, I think of strawberry jam. It does seem strange. Yes, the human mind is capable of tricks.

"Mama.

"Mama, let me hold your hand.

"Mama is upset, sir. I can tell. She is thinking of the time we stole some strawberry jam. But, just then, when I was putting it on some bread, the men came. The two with machine guns had thick eyebrows. I remember that. They were like wolves. If there had been time to growl and show their teeth, they would have done just that. But since they had machine guns slung over their shoulders, they didn't have to. They just nuzzled us as though we were kittens; and we obeyed.

"Maybe, instead of eating strawberry jam, we should have been making machine guns to put in the windows facing out to the world. Then . . . ratatattat. Who's there? Rat-a-tat-tat. That would have been a proper answer. . . ."

Forgive me thinking aloud, dear friend. I wandered off again. It was nothing. Nothing at all. Really.

My daughter? It is late, is it not? We've walked a good distance. I am weary. No, no, I'm quite all right. I should retire. Another time, if you choose. I would be delighted.

Your patience, your forbearance, sir, have been more than I expected or deserved. I hardly dared hope that you would return today and ask at what time we can meet tomorrow; you are more than kind. Whenever you say. Early? Yes. I sleep lightly. As early as dawn? Yes, I too like to walk at that hour. We are having a spell of extraordinary weather. Not a cloud in the sky.

May I leave you here, then? No, you take the first taxi. I would, for a moment, like to step inside these Cathedral doors. A magnificent monument to the spirit of man, is it not? Carved, it seems out of the very rock upon which this island rests. A haven in the midst of man's earthly toils; a sanctuary for the weary-souled and the hard of heart. May I light a candle for you, sir? By all means. It would give me a great deal of pleasure. . . . Here, then, at dawn? An ideal choice. It would be most convenient for myself. Farewell, then, cher ami. And, please convey my kindest wishes to your fiancée.

CHAPTER V

Good morning, sir! I do feel much better. You, too, look rested. As you had been concerned about my weariness, as we parted in the evening, I, too, had begun to feel some concern for yourself. You had begun to show a sign of strain.

A beautiful morning, yes. Would you care to step inside for a moment before we begin our walk? I did light a candle for you last night. I spent a most peaceful hour within. There was a full choir for vespers service. Not a few stood in line when it was over with to enter an antechamber, presumably for communion. I might have, yes; however, I have an aversion to lines. Another time, perhaps.

You say you watched television? A western? I am acquainted with them. And, I enjoy them. They are diverting and entertaining, and quite soothing to one's nerves after the bustle of an anxious day. Oh, yes, there are critics, to be sure, who run on at great length, about the immorality of the shooting and what not, insisting that they are hardly true to life, and that they corrupt the morals of children, frightening them into nightmares and brutalizing their instincts. A bit far-fetched, wouldn't you say, in the light of . . . re-cent history? These critics would take the very joy out of life itself. They, too soon, forget that they once were children. You are right. These guardians of our morals forget the most essential element of these simple western stories—that they do portray the individual hero capable of making a moral choice, even if, at times, the plot might be some-what contrived, or oversimplified.

I suppose they do have a point in that the matter of good and evil is not quite so simple and children should not be so misled. And, they might be quite right in going to such lengths to indicate that the desperado standing at the bar, challenging another to the draw, is not necessarily a bad man. Who knows; perhaps he had not been fed his mother's milk as an infant, or perhaps, he had been set out to fend for himself at an early age. And, indeed, the man who gets shot down in the duel had, of course, driven the aggressor to such lengths; so you see, he is not altogether innocent. There have been recent discoveries in numerous fields of thought and science which can prove quite categor-ically that each of us is driven by hidden desires and thoughts, and that if one does commit a crime, he is not at all responsible for it because, for the moment, he was subject to these hidden drives. And one can prove very readily that guilt is divisible. Whether right or wrong, it is a most convenient thought for our times, and one might almost say that the discovery or formulation of the thought had helped to prepare for our era. You see, we've come to deplore the simple tale of good and evil in terms of a child's native culture because such simplicity would hardly suffice for . . . other matters.

An unpleasant subject, to be sure, on such a glorious morning. Shall we then head for the river to get a glimpse of the eastern sun casting her gold upon the ships of the harbor? Even these behemoths of industry, along the other shore, take on an enchantment quite their own in the early morning light. The air is not yet laden with smoke from those gigantic chimneys. The shadows they cast at this early hour are never sinister. The machine, in a state of sleep, as you have probably noticed, being an early riser like myself, has a naked beauty worthy of the trained artist's eye, like the regal harlot, who, in her sleep, with arms outstretched and a milk-white bosom glistening in the morning sun, calls us to her warm embrace.

Yes, I have had my morning coffee. And you,

sir? I would enjoy another if you have not. You would rather walk? My daughter? Did we find her? No. Not exactly. We had news of her. Or, I should better say, we thought we had news of her. I really should not have said "we," because I stood, unfortunately, quite alone in the matter. An estrangement had begun between my dear wife and myself. For whatever reasons, we saw little of each other. Her duties at the hospital had become more pressing; and where, at first, she might spend an occasional night there, she had soon begun to spend weeks there without returning home.

As I said, I did finally have word of my daughter, although the visit in which news of her was related to me was not really about her at all, dealing, rather, with a totally different matter. An acquaintance—a man whom I had met upon occasion at a mutual acquaintance's home; ah, yes, I believe I mentioned her before, the ravishing woman for whom men had purchased such fabulous jewels—a man who had once been a University professor, not that this would necessarily set him apart, came to call. He was, at the time, holding a rather high position in our government. And although you might, at first, think of him as a collaborator, serving in a government which had no kind of latitude in either domestic or foreign affairs, I can assure you that he was a patriot, in every sense. Chance, you see, had left him behind in these troubled times. Others of his own rank, as statesmen, from various parties, had been more or less fortunate, as the case may be, in having found sanctuary upon foreign soil, in advance of the conqueror's forces, where they remained vocal patriots to the very end. Not a few, however, had been forced by circumstances to remain behind, and had accepted, with some reluctance, positions commensurate with their rank, to help, in whatever way possible, to alleviate the stifling nature of the occupation.

Yes, I agree. History will judge them one way or another. In some cases, as you must be aware, its long arm has, to put it mildly, shorn a few of somewhat more than their hair.

He had a vague knowledge of my daughter's whereabouts. Anxious, if not demanding queries from myself were of little avail. Couldn't I see her then? Could I not then communicate with her? Surely, then, you will arrange for my wife to carry her something baked by her own hand. My entreaties not only went unheeded, but hardly listened to. His own daughter, as well as his son-in-law, was being detained under similar circumstances; and he knew no more of them than of my daughter. He surmised that they were alive . . . at the moment.

I, as three others had been, besides the gentleman of whom I am speaking, was being asked to assume an obligation as . . . a citizen of some standing, which would be beneficial to everyone concerned; especially to our own countrymen. We were being asked, or better yet importuned, to act as a Commission of Inquiry into certain allegations that the voluntary labor camp at Auschwitz had a defective sanitary system; and that, in some instances, there had been abuses of authority on the part of the administration. It seems that slanderous rumors were being circulated, by a secret newspaper, which implied a good deal more than abuse of authority, and firm denials over a long period of time by the proper authorities had been of little avail, and unless the propaganda, which had become more vitriolic and irresponsible by the week, ceased, certain punitive measures would have to be taken. It was felt that such a Commission of Inquiry, making a thorough investigation and reporting it in full, would undermine the slanders. In turn, if my daughter was being held—and, of course, one would have to accept their word in the matter, she might in exchange for the service rendered, be allowed to return to her home in a probationary status.

"In short, sir," I replied, "it is obvious that conditions are being placed upon us in order that we report whatever they deem it proper to report."

"Not at all," averred the gentleman of high place. "Not at all. I have their guarantee that we shall be allowed to report what we see, to the last detail."

"Why, then, do they use our children as hostages if there is no pressure being exerted. Under these circumstances, I refuse. I mean no offense to yourself. None at all. But, to put it bluntly, we are being coerced."

I need not tell you that he was chagrined; hurt. He insisted that I did not understand a responsibility I had.

I was taken aback. I became firm. "Sir," I pleaded, "you should understand that my own daughter considered me lacking in patriotism and refused to speak to me. My wife has had little if anything to do with me since my daughter's disappearance. I have come to a decision which is irrevocable. Even if I cannot fight, I insist that I will not, in any way, henceforth abet the occupation of our country."

He was moved. He said he admired my forthright position and that under most circumstances it would be thought highly of and I would be considered a patriot. However, I had overlooked an obligation I had to my fellow-man beyond our own borders. Was it not important for the five of us to take the opportunity afforded to enter the camp and to study it in full detail so that we might keep a record for the world of what we had seen? "Would you not consider this a higher patriotism than refusing?"

He studied me intently to see whether I did not show some wavering of my previous firmness. If I did not reflect in my countenance an unease, I can assure you that I was not inwardly calm. My mind had wandered to Calais and to those famous Burghers the artist Rodin had sculpted into a lasting fame, who, to save their city from a sacking by the invading force, agreed to give up their lives; and bidding farewell to their loved ones carried the key to Calais out to the foe, knowing that they were to meet a certain death. You are familiar with the work? Rodin captured them at that moment of decision, starting on their march with a dignity and a nobility worthy of the occasion! A great work of art! Yes, there is some history connected with it to that effect. The Queen, moved by their courage, did intervene and the Burghers, I believe, were released. The King's heart was not made entirely of stone.

What did I respond to the man who would head the Commission? Nothing. There was no need to say anything at all. There was not, in reality, any kind of choice. As he studied my countenance for my reaction to his placing the matter in the light of a responsibility to future generations, he added, quite calmly and matter-of-factly, that it had been made very clear to him that should we find it impossible to comply with the request, we would be invited to Auschwitz in another capacity. There was a contingent leaving the following even-ing, all of whom had volunteered their labor most willingly, and since there were five places that had not been assigned, we would be allowed to volun-teer for them.

"I am sure you can understand their intent," he went on. "They do mean to have us go. And, although I am loathe to suggest your own decision to yourself, I would strongly advise your consent in the matter, since, as I said before, an impression of this place must and should be recorded. It may very well be," he went on, "that the rumors are not altogether true about . . . certain things and that the underground is exaggerating in order to arouse the people. As you are aware, in times of war, some incidents, or events, are magnified, understandably of course, since it is morale which is the deciding factor, assuming that the combatants are evenly matched in arms. You should, if you can spare the time, help to assume a responsibility which I feel we have. I must, however, have an answer by morning. Should you decide that you will go, merely drop this white card, which has my address on it, in my letter box. If I don't find the card by—shall we say, nine o'clock—I shall be obliged to take care of some very urgent matters of state and dictate a few memoranda of one kind or another before evening, since I have not been allowed any kind of latitude in the matter of choice. In short, I am not able to replace you. Unless the five of us consent to go, the Commission will be considered dissolved." And with this, he parted.

Look, sir, the city is awakening. The longshoremen are being assigned their morning chores. An ancient and a most noble calling, would you not say? One might, indeed, while lifting upon his shoulders a hundredweight of coffee, exuding the aroma of distant lands, fall into a quiet and most enchanting reverie; just as his stevedore counterpart in distant lands must, as he enters the hold, dream of far fairer shores than his own, cursing, perhaps, the bronze-skinned lass upon whose bosom he had shed tears the night before for her duplicity in being liberal with her charms, envying his northern counterpart who lives on streets paved with gold, who can, if he chooses, set forth in a wagon train and carve himself an empire on western plains, or indeed marry his employer's daughter and become a captain plying the seven seas; and our own longshoreman, this morning, as he first steps into that very same hold, transforms the luxurious odor of fresh coffee into a bronze-skinned damsel who waits for his counterpart on shore, ready to lead him by the hand into neighboring streets festooned for the Mardi Gras, the enchanting music finds him dancing with yet another exotic, masked woman who not only falls in love with him, but, despite his lowly station, commands his hand and takes him home to her father's hacienda, hidden in a forest of coffee trees, the ripened fruit being picked to the drumbeat rhythm of native music, the master of the plantation, himself, joining in the festivity of the harvest.

I do not jest, at all, my friend. Would that I had been a longshoreman at either place on that very evening of which I had been speaking. For as he left me, there I stood, staring at the grim white card he had placed in my hand; and as I studied it, I am sure I saw a rank X marked upon it in black ink, which I had not noticed before.

What did I do? I thought urgently about the matter. I tried to reach my wife but was informed that she was in surgery and since there was a steady stream of emergency cases, she would not be available that night. I went to visit the young lady of whom I've spoken, to ask her advice. She was not at home and was not expected for several months to come.

And then what? I prepared myself for the coming venture as best I could. Surely, sir, you are jesting? Perhaps I failed to convey to you, in the telling, in what manner the question was placed. The underground? Why didn't I try to make contact with them? Ah, cher ami, would that by some miracle or blessing they had appeared, from wherever they were, and dispatched with a Molotov cocktail . . . forgive me, a grenade, the two automobiles that stood across from my place, both of which, as though driven by some unseen hand, had followed me on my brief excursions to the hospital and my friend's home. I was, to put it bluntly, under surveillance.

Having come to a decision, I set to work with that kind of plan, persistence and detail that had characterized my attitude towards my profession. I was quite surprised how an inward calm returned once I had thrust myself into my work. Even though the gentlemen were across the street watching the house, and I could deduct, of course, that they were posted at several vantage points about the grounds, I temporarily lost my fear. I had heard, as you very likely had, (I'm sorry, I forget that you must have been quite young then) of that famous slogan which was painted across the top of the arbor-like gate of the very place we were being invited to visit, *Arbeit Macht Frei,* "work gives freedom," and I must confess that, in thinking of it, I held the man who worded the thought in the highest esteem. The moment I had set to work to prepare for dropping the card in the letter box and setting out on what would very likely be an uncomfortable automobile journey, I began to feel a most salutary soaring of the spirit, as though I were

actually free. I began to sing, quite loudly, anything that came into my mind, such as the song of
our conqueror's airforce (I recalled the young chap
who liked Renoir so much) or some older lieder
with which the gentlemen parked across the street
could not have been unfamiliar. This, as you can
readily see, was a mask. I had a task to perform
which should not arouse any curiosity out of the
ordinary.

My jewels? They were important and had to
be put in a proper place for safekeeping. But they,
all of them, could be duplicated in one way or
another; it would take but a practised eye and an
ancient skill handed down through the ages—a skill
and a knowledge which was mine. However, the
one jewel which that ancient had left with me in
exchange for his child's life, that jewel, I knew I
could not duplicate. And I was intent upon finding a place suitable to preserving its majestic quality for somewhat longer than what had been
indicated as a brief journey of inquiry, just in case
we had motor trouble on the return trip. One
could not depend upon one's means of conveyance
in these troubled times.

After having taken a complete inventory of all
I had in stock and placing them in their cases

within a vaulted wall safe of some size, located behind a wonderful replica of Courbet's *La Source* (aside from my own appreciation for it as a work of art, I had always felt that whoever looked at it would become engrossed enough to forego searching behind it)—after completing this task which I had done many times before, I went into my private study, in which the heavy drapes were already drawn (I did not wish to draw any blinds while they were watching, lest they have their curiosity aroused—it seemed best, under such circumstances, to act as unconcerned as one might were he sitting on his front porch reading the newspaper) and closed the door behind me. It did not take me long to prepare the place which I knew would be suitable for the jewel. I had, without quite realizing it, prepared in my subconscious mind for such an eventuality, and you might say, I had dreamed it into existence. You've had that experience, I'm sure. You've been doing an equation in mathematics, fretting over it for hours on end, and have, upon retiring, fallen into a state of half-sleep, half-wake, in which you've dreamed the solution to the vexing problem. This had happened to myself without realizing it. I had carried the precious jewel into the study without thinking about it.

There, my eye was drawn to a particular stone in the fireplace wall, above which hung a painting of Christ portrayed as a hunchback, which I had picked up at an auction for less than the cost of the canvas on which it was painted. The painter had never been heard of, although I had showed it to numerous art dealers. It was almost by chance that I found the author's inscription in a corner of it, the painting having to be held in a particular light for it to be visible. One had a feeling, as he tried to make out the letters of the name, that this unknown painter had so interwoven his soul with the work, that he little cared whether anyone knew his name or not. And, although these same art dealers had not thought highly of the work, considering it eclectic in form, lacking individuality of style, and criticizing it on numerous other grounds as lacking in proportion as to all of the accepted rules of the art of painting, having too much darkness as opposed to light, the two being quite out of balance, etc.; I nonetheless felt that this unknown painter had captured a particular expression which I had always felt Our Lord must have had during those moments he was carrying the Cross upon his back. And I prized it greatly.

The stone, to which my eye was drawn, as

though the idea had been preconceived, was the very stone upon which the eyes of this Christ figure were focused. I set to work to cut it out of the masonry with my finest tools, careful to leave no trace of disturbance around its edges. It would be almost impossible to describe to you my amazement in finding, upon removal of the stone, a crypt-like vault that seemed to have been left on purpose for this jewel. The artisan who had worked upon this wall had had such mastery of his craft that he had, as any good mason does, left unnoticeable passages through the masonry which permitted an adequate circulation of air from without. The crypt behind the stone had been left as a breathing space for this whole wall!

My work finished, with the stone replaced, I left a note to my wife in a crack which lay behind an exposed beam on the cellar stairway—a place agreed upon many months before should we be unable to communicate with each other through any other means, explaining to her by what light and in precisely what place she would have to stand to see the focus of the eyes in the painting upon that stone behind which the precious jewel lay.

The next morning, I left that grim white card,

with the rank X showing plainly on it, in the letter box before the appointed hour.

Ah, sir, I believe this gentleman is the numbers man, plying his trade along the docks, as cheap as a penny for a chance. I am told that one can sometimes win as much as five hundred times the amount he places in lottery. Are you good at numbers? Shall we chance a pennyeach? My good man, may we have a number? Ah, thank you. You write in your booklet with care. A penny for my friend! Here you are! And, now my own. You pick it for me. I must select my own? 118,700. Too large? Then, anything you say. You can give me the last three if I like? Excellent! Your pencil writes in what appears to be an indelible ink. What if our receipt is lost? Would it not be safer to tattoo our number on our forearm? Then, should some act of God (perish the thought) lay you abed before the lottery is over, we will, should we lose our paper and should our number be drawn, have indisputable claim to the prize. No need of that? You say you will remember us by our faces? Wonderful! My penny, then! A most remarkable game! And you, sir, are a most admirable man that can remember a fellow man for as little as a penny bet!

CHAPTER VI

The trip? We left that afternoon, quite late, in a chauffeured automobile, built conveniently to carry five passengers in comfort. One does not see that kind of sedan much anymore, with those folding seats in the back, designed for such state occasions.

With dispatch, and perfect ease of handling, our chauffeur guided us through narrow streets into the main highway leading south out of Warsaw. If we had been steering a compass course and I chose to be more exact in describing the route, I would have to say he drove southwest. It mattered little enough. When the sun is to your right as you travel and it is near to setting, you know that you travel south, and each of us knew that in this direction lay Auschwitz.

"Our countryside is grey, but beautiful," said one of my fellow passengers, thumbing a worn briefcase held between his knees, a man whose business in gravestones had fallen off, and who had taken up his former craft of stonecarver.

"I understand," said another, drawing with a trained hand upon a pad before him, a man who had been a manufacturer of caskets and had a national reputation for the superb individual design carved upon each as a fitting epitaph for the deceased, "we are going to have a poor harvest this year. It seems that the weather. . . . "

"Yes, it was an unseasonably cool summer. This makes a difference," said our Chairman, a former professor of languages.

"However," said a priest, another of our Commission, "if winter is here, spring cannot be far behind . . . another growing season will begin."

"What, Rudin," asked the head of our Commission of myself, "would you like to be, if you could have your whole life to live over again?"

"Of one thing only can I be sure," I answered with some gravity, "and that is that no matter what else I did, I would take an active interest in my country's politics." I received a sudden blow on my shins, which I misunderstood to have come from a shuffling of feet. "Indeed," I went on, "with no offense intended for ourselves as representatives, in a sense, of government, I would have taken more than an active interest. I would have seen to it that we had been prepared for . . . " and I received another, more painful kick.

My friends quickly changed the subject to the matter of the new synthetic rubber factory that was being built at the voluntary labor camp which we were to visit, a most worthy enterprise; and how, one day, through the efficiency and the genius for organization of those who were presently in command, the foundations will have been laid for a city of the future. The cost, it was true, might prove to be great, and not a few would give their lives, the region being swampy and unhealthy by nature, a common peasant saying about the area being, "it was avoided by life for a thousand years as death kept watch there," which made the effort that much the more remarkable.

It was not long before we passed a lengthy caravan of trucks traveling the same highway, which, from a distance, one would pay little attention to, assuming that cattle were heading for a southern market, a not unnatural sight when one was traveling this thoroughfare. However, as we passed them by, a quick turn of our eyes (our chauffeur was adept at driving with one eye on the road before him and the other on his rearview mirror) revealed a child's hand protruding through a narrow slit in one of them; and one could deduce that the trucks were assisting gypsies in their travels to a southern climate, since winter was already here.

I had been smoking my cigarette (as you can see, I am what you call a chain smoker) and had been dropping my ashes into a tray before me, which, like any ordinary automotive ashtray, had a round metal loop through which to drop them, and, as I say, although not unlike any ordinary tray, the ash-catcher was unusual enough in design to catch my eye from time to time; and as I was about to exclaim about the child's hand, this ash-catcher drew my eye again. I suddenly realized what had been so unique about the design and why it had so drawn my practiced jeweler's eye. I regretted having left my eyepiece in my desk. This catcher was, indeed, somewhat suggestive of the human ear. Remarkable, I thought, and most diverting! A fellow craftsman who had not, even in our age of mass production and war, lost his feeling for his craft.

Fascinated as I was, and anxious to know the name and address of such an artist, I was about to tap upon the window separating our riding compartment from the chauffeur, to ask if he might have such information, when the woman member of our Commission, an operatic soprano of some repute in European concert halls, broke into song and bade us join her in a chorus, an opportunity one did not decline, for surely, it was not every day that one could sit beside and sing with someone of such renown and talent. As you can see, our troubled times did have their compensations. If before, one had had to pay a premium price, or even bribe a friend of a friend, to gain admission to hear a concert, let alone make the acquaintance of an artist of such rank and genius, during the years of which I speak, one might find himself riding the same compartment. The men who planned such occasions were, you see, democratic in their outlook.

The songs did brighten our journey considerably, for the skies were a dismal grey. Occasionally, one might be distracted by a passing column of helmeted and bayoneted soldiers, marching in perfect time to songs of their own choosing, who would, waving to us as we passed them by, reflect envy in their countenance. Marching afoot is not necessarily the most comfortable way to make a long journey.

Or, one might see an occasional resorter, on a southern trip, drawing one of those conveyances that have become so popular in your country—I believe you call them house-trailers? These were well designed, with venetian blinded windows on the side, through which it seemed one might peer into the privacy of a home, but as one drew close, one noticed that they were painted—a most ingenious camouflage, with real windows hard to get; necessary in order that the owner of such a vehicle would not feel inferior because he could not afford to pay the blackmarket price for real ones. And, to save the cost of any special heating equipment, a hose extended from the exhaust of his trucklike auto into his trailer. The driver could, when he alighted, have a fully heated van in which he could fall into a restful and much deserved sleep. If there were a few deathly fumes that might have passed from the exhaust into this Valhalla on wheels, there was, above the window, a ventilating fan to air it out. In our troubled times, everything was being done for our weary vacationer's comfort and ease of mind.

Would you care for a late breakfast? The restaurants hereabouts, I see, are not what one would call select. But then, if one limits himself in his choice of foods, he should not suffer any kind of indigestion. I see that our hearty longshoremen demonstrate a happy appetite in this place. Shall we then?

Ah, sir, a fine table next to the window. The view from the bridge here is excellent. That long-shoreman across the way looks familiar, bargaining with that gentleman about his fate. Do you ever play the game of guessing people's names? What do you say to our giving it a try? Let's wager on that longshoreman first. He looks American; tough, angry. What would you say? George? I agree, too common. Shall we try John? No, it doesn't fit that jutting jaw. What say you to Ed? Shall we try it? We'll ask him if he comes across. The gentleman with him, standing near the phone booth, is pouring it on, as you say here. They are having a real go at it. Someone is telling a tale.

The winsome lass in her becoming waitress's frock is waiting for our order. What will you have? Only black coffee? Do have something more. The walk must surely have famished you. Have you ever tried fried eggs over easy on a stack of griddle cakes? It sounds awful? Really! I learned that in America. Look over yonder to the counter. You see? I wasn't wrong. You, my young man, have not lived, as the saying goes. Where do you keep yourself? Surely, you do not breakfast on oatmeal and cream alone! While there's food to be had, one should not disdain it, even at the cost of being a pound or two overweight. Will you try it then? Two of the same, my dear. Your maple syrup, too; pure maple.

Did you notice her magnificent bosom as she cleared the table? The proprietor of this cafe thinks highly of his clientele and has a keen eye for detail. I hope, sir, I don't embarrass you. Really, I didn't mean to be crude. You are blushing. I did enjoy looking at her magnificent breasts as she bent over the table. Ah, I believe you picture to yourself a European who delights in pinching young women on the behind. I assure you, in all seriousness, I've never had so bad a habit. I see that I did embarrass you. I apologize. I may have spoken crudely. I was thinking, I must confess, as I studied their contour, of the joy she gives to her lover as he fondles them. I do admire the human form, male and female; and if I prefer to gaze upon the latter more, it's because I am the former, and quite normal in my instincts. I do always doff my cap at a majestic bosom, for the sheer magnificence of its existence. . . . The human form, sir . . . I was thinking of it, yes . . . as something . . . not to be desecrated. I always fear falling into abstractions, or even what your critics might call rhetoric. If one were to say outright, "the human form, it should not be desecrated . . . "—imagine what would happen to one of your playwrights if he were to say such a thing in a play. Just supposing he put those words into the mouth of an actor at a critical moment of high tragedy, "the human form shouldn't be desecrated." He'd be hooted and howled to failure by your critics as a moralist and as a writer of didactic rhetoric. Supposing he went on and said . . . "there were human forms that ceased to be human forms . . . who did things to the human form . . . terrible things;" there, if he were to blurt it out like that and describe it point blank, he would be accused of much worse than rhetoric. That's why if one of your famous Southern dramatists has most of his heroines appearing on stage in a slip, he cannot be accused at all of exploiting sex. He is merely demonstrating the beauty of the human form and we should be grateful.

Ah, yes, that's what is always said—the human form is not always beautiful; there are few women who approach the Venus de Milo. We will not dispute the matter. Even the misbegotten hold in their mind's eye a vision of Venus, and if that one moment comes when the wretched and the ugly behold beauty in their beloved, they have found grace. And this happens! Ah, sir, you will force me to rhetoric yet.

I am sorry I digressed. I can understand your impatience. But, you see, the matter of her graceful and majestic bosom was not altogether a digression. You are interested in the cold hard facts of the matter. Auschwitz! It rolls off your tongue easily. I'm sorry, I offended you. I shouldn't have said that.

The gate was festooned for our arrival with shipped in flowers of every hot house variety; and from a distance, above the miasmatic yellow fog that rubbed itself upon the auto's window panes and hovered like a specter over the countryside, that sign, *Arbeit Macht Frei,* was visible. Those buildings which were in close to the gateway were quite invisible for the fog, thus not distracting from three tall chimneys which must have been more than a mile or two in the distance rising to a lofty height above the horizon.

The woman member of our Commission, now quite hoarse from the extended concert she had given for us through the greater part of the night, said, "Goodness, I'll catch my death of cold," as she drew her fur about her neck. And any trepidation we might have felt as we alighted before the assistant commandant's quarters were soon dispelled, as he broke the solemnity of the moment by proffering a kiss upon the hand of our star, and in a most courteous manner, introduced himself as SS Hauptsturmführer . . . at our service. He let us know without hesitation that he had strict orders from the Commandant to let us see anything we chose. The day and Auschwitz were ours! The Commandant had sent his profuse apologies for being unable to conduct us on a tour himself, but insisted that we be his guests at dinner that evening.

"Your arrival was indeed timely," stated our guide without more ado. "We've had a disturbance in blockhouse thirty during the night and one of our charges was found murdered in bed. If we have to delay our inquiry into the sanitation system for an hour or so, you will find it worth your while . . . our administration of justice here. We do not condone murder We have, however, as you will see, many unscrupulous devils who would do their fellow man in for a pittance. In short, we have, as any growing community does, some who commit premeditated murder, which makes our task much more difficult. As you can understand, one cannot expect more when we have so mixed a population. Hardly a country of Europe has not volunteered labor for our enterprise here, and as you know from your own experience, there are, under such circumstances, ill-bred ruffians who have sneaked in, as it were. Shall we then? To blockhouse thirty. Your car will drive you."

"A question, if I may, SS Hauptsturmführer. . . ."

"You may call me Colonel, if you choose," said our guide.

"Colonel; your fencing. There are two of them. Why should there be need of two fences, if labor here is voluntary?"

"Ah," smiled the Colonel. "An acute observation. The fences are not intended, as you can readily see, to keep those who are in, in; but rather, to keep those who are out, out. There has been, as you have unquestionably noticed, even in Warsaw, a serious dislocation of the economy and jobs are somewhat scarce. We have had many who have tried to get in, when we would not have jobs for them. In fact, there was nothing less than an armed attack upon our compound less than a month ago. That's why those towers at several locations are manned with machine guns and expert marksmen. You see, of the two fences, only the outer is charged with current around the clock. The inner one is currentless by day, charged at night. This way, we conserve electric power. I must confess, I erred, when you arrived. I believe I said the Commandant stated you might go wherever you wish, without exception. There is an exception, however, but it's not really considered an exception because it's been always understood as one and henceforth one doesn't consider it when one speaks of one's freedom to go where he chooses. That group of buildings, some two hundred yards to your left, enclosed with the stake fencing, we would prefer that you accept a gentleman's agreement" (and here he bowed slightly to the single woman member of our Commission, out of respect) "not to ask to visit that portion of the compound."

"Why?" asked our reverend father. "It was understood that we would see everything."

"Out of respect to your sensibilities, father," responded our Colonel. "I assure you, you would find that particular group of buildings quite uninteresting; and I'm sure you'll find more than enough to occupy you, since our sanitation system is quite complex. I must hurry, if you will, to blockhouse thirty. We've detained them from work; and this means docking their wages, and if we don't complete the matter at hand, finding who committed a foul deed during the night, we'll soon have a loud grumble to be sure."

"But Colonel, it is with some dismay, to be sure, that you inform us before we have hardly arrived that a portion of your compound is out of bounds to a Commission of Inquiry," said our Chairman. "That bit of news does not rest well at all. It would seem, if we are going to try to give you a clean bill of health, a gold star rating, as it were, those buildings will have to be open for inspection."

"Surely, Mr. Chairman," responded our guide with a detached congeniality, "all of us have little secrets we must keep, even though we never speak of them as such. It was my error in having told you that all of Auschwitz lay at your disposal. If you will forgive my repeating myself, I should not have spoken of an exception, since it really isn't an exception, being readily accepted as an exception, thus not really one. We are delaying justice. Even the most respectable families, and I'm sure there are not exceptions to the rule of thumb, our present party, even including myself not excepted, have a skeleton in the closet, and civilized sensibilities do accept the exception without really speaking of it as one. It is amazing what we know of each other, is it not? For example, of yourself, Mr. Chairman, there was a matter . . . not long ago. . . . "

"Really," I broke in here, with some firmness, knowing to what the Colonel might refer, "I believe you are exceeding yourself, Colonel. I believe that we may accept, for now, at least, the gentleman's agreement about that portion of the compound. We may be forced to raise the matter with the Commandant himself. But tell me, dear Colonel, those chimneys, so well proportioned, rising to such dizzying heights at the far end of the compound, what are they? They dominate your low-lying landscape, as it were. You might say, indeed, that one could almost touch them, yet my better sense tells me they are two or three miles distant."

"Your ability to judge distance is phenomenal. They are roughly two miles away. They are really not part of this particular compound, although administratively speaking, they are. They serve the final processing plant at Birkenau, and, as a matter of fact, those chimneys were completed not too long ago. We have increased production considerably and if you have some knowledge of chemistry and synthetics, you will understand the need for such tall chimneys. That being the final processing plant to which all materials go, you understand, I am sure, the relationship between synthetics and decomposition—the height of the chimneys assures clean air about. In short, if I might be crude, the odors from the processes are somewhat fierce, if not sulphurous. Short chimneys, when the winds were still, or if they moved in this direction, made the air quite impure for breathing. The taller the chimney, the further the smoke is carried across the countryside."

"I see," said our carver of caskets, "that your furnaces are going at full blast this morning."

"Yes," smiled our Colonel. "Our production schedules are uninterrupted, as it were. Although most of the compound sleeps through the night, the final processing plant works around the clock. Otherwise we couldn't keep up with production demands. Shall we then?"

"I say, Colonel," asked our singer, whose voice had collected itself, "that framework your carpenters are building in that square?"

"Ah, madame. I really would prefer that another tell you. Perhaps your Chairman will, as you drive to blockhouse thirty." And, with this, the Colonel whispered into our Chairman's ear, who listened intently, as we took the moment's respite to gaze longingly to that portion of the compound which was out of bounds. And, as we were studying it, a squad of workers could be seen marching at a four count in the distance. One of the marchers, who seemed to be suffering from sore feet fell by the wayside momentarily, and the Kapo (this was the squad leader, as I later learned) bade the column halt, that he might render first aid, using nothing less than his own unsoiled handkerchief to bind his charge's left foot, patting him encouragingly on the shoulder, a kindly gesture from a younger to an older man. Then, as the older man limped back to his place four abreast, the Kapo bade two of the more stalwart looking men give the older one a helping hand, slowing his four count measure to a pace suitable for him.

Ah, our longshoreman is coming in the door. You guessed the name of Ed. Shall we ask him? I beg your pardon, sir. We played a game as you stood across the street near the phone booth, your well dressed friend attempting to bar your entrance. Were we correct in conjecturing the name of Ed? We were right? Your friends call you Eddie!

Would you care to join us for some coffee? Our apologies. Yes, it is a silly game for grown men at the break of dawn.

He speaks straight from the shoulder. I should have taken all of the blame. It was, after all, my idea.

Did you enjoy your hearty breakfast? I'm glad you did. Do you take a cigar this early in the morning? You prefer your pipe? I prefer my Havana, yes.

Our acquaintance, Eddie, is staring at us. What say you to a brisk walk? Are you game? I believe he mistook our game for something else. He is possessed of a suspicious frame of mind.

After you, cher ami. Good morning, my dear. Yes, I did enjoy the breakfast very much. And, your smiling countenance. You may expect me on the morrow at this same time for breakfast. I would like to, if I may, bring a flawless necklace to present to you, if you can assure me the owner of the cafe will not consider it amiss. And, I shall look forward to the moment when you set my place with appreciation. May I then kiss your hand? Ah, come now. They are not dishwater hands, and please don't hold them behind you so shyly. It would give me great pleasure and I would consider myself honored. Our advertisers who blemish a young lady's character by plaguing her with such rude insult, suggesting that someone as lovely as yourself has despoiled herself by washing dishes, should be punished with the bastinado. Your hands, in truth, my dear, are as lovely as your bosom, and if what I say seems brazen, I ask that you accept my apologies.

Until tomorrow then.

CHAPTER VII

I see I did embarrass you. You are laughing. I'm sure now you take me for a rake. You believe that my concern for the human form is a guise; that I present a front to you; that if the opportunity arose I would pinch a young lady beneath the table.

And that silly game, guessing a man's name. It seemed childish to you, did it not? The stern visage of the longshoreman did make us appear quite out of place, I agree. I have, however, a strange obsession for names.

The scaffold being built in the square at Auschwitz? Our Chairman informed us as we rode to blockhouse thirty that it was a gallows. Our Colonel, it seems, deplored the very thought of a gallows and found it most unseeming to speak of it before the woman member of our Commission. The Commandant did not condone murder at Auschwitz and demanded a summary apprehension and punishment of the guilty one. The hanging would take place at sunset of that day before the whole compound as a warning to all would-be miscreants.

As we approached blockhouse thirty my gaze was taken by that same column of fours which had stopped at blockhouse twenty-eight (and but for the fact that they were numbered, one would not have known which was which, for the architect who designed the barrack-like structures had been advised to take the strictest economic measures, thus having all of the beams and cross-beams of equal length; the single door and windows of the same size; the length, width and all measurements the same; and if the architect would not for this work achieve international distinction, he was commended for the money he saved in time of war). The older gentleman who had been given first aid by the Kapo was being assisted by two younger men into house twenty-eight, but a short distance away, and I was struck by a strange sensation of recognition. I was sure I knew that man and bade the Chairman of our Commission to proceed with the inquiry in blockhouse thirty while I ambled over to pay my respects to number twenty-eight.

"If you insist," said our Chairman. "But, be so good as to check the plumbing while you're there. It will save us much needed time."

"I will," I answered, making note of the matter. "And, please give my apologies to the SS

Hauptsturmführer," as I proceeded to make my call.

It was on the short walk of fifty or a hundred yards, while examining a flower bed before blockhouse number twenty-nine, that my eye was caught by a boot, thrust upward through the soil, despoiling an otherwise quite orderly garden upon which someone had lavished unusual care. Although no flowers were then in bloom, it being winter, one could see from the vital roots of the pruned roses, cut back to the ground, that the soil beneath was rich. My trade, of course, being jewels, I could not speak with authority on the matter, but from what I had seen growing in our own garden when fertilizer was hard to get, I could surmise that this soil was not deprived of food. Obviously, some careless person had heaved his boot out the window of the blockhouse, caring little where it landed. I made a note of it for the Commandant and walked to where it lay to carry it back to the doorstep of twenty-nine, where its rightful, but temperamental owner, might claim it. Alas, sir, it would not budge. The ground seemed to be frozen about it and would not relinquish the boot. Tug on the foot of it as I might, it would not unhinge itself from its moorings; and the harder I gripped it, the more solidly filled it seemed, as though the dirt from beneath, heaving up, as often happens with soil in repeated frosts and thaws, had filled the boot quite full.

I walked to the men of the column of fours, some two hundred, standing at attention, waiting for their Kapo. Never in my life had I seen such ragged specimens of humankind. Aside from the jaundiced skin and the eyes jutting from skeletal frames their clothes were utterly unkempt. They looked straight before them not deigning to notice me.

"I beg your pardon, gentlemen, but it seems I've found a boot lying in the rosebed at the side of blockhouse number twenty-nine. Could one of you have left it there by chance?"

They didn't respond. Not one. I walked up to the one closest and asked in somewhat firmer voice. "My good man. There's a boot lying there. No one seems to take an interest. Would you, by any chance, know who the owner of that fine boot might be?"

Again silence. The Kapo had come out of number thirty.

"You are from the Commission of Inquiry, I

trust?" said the Kapo. "May I be of some assistance?"

"Yes. A boot. I found a boot lying in the rosebed of number twenty-nine, frozen into the ground, as it were. I was enquiring of these gentlemen if they knew to whom it belonged."

"Ah, yes. The boot outside of twenty-nine."

"I thought I'd call it to the attention of the Commandant."

"The Commandant knows of that boot, sir. It must remain where it is. It is a marker. It is being kept as evidence."

"I see."

"Yes, as evidence. It has been photographed. Soundings have been made. There lies a tale beneath that boot."

"I see. Our Chairman must know of this then."

"By all means," responded the Kapo.

"The gentleman whom you've taken into number twenty-eight there. I thought I recognized him. Might I pay him a call?"

"By all means. He would appreciate that."

"May I then?"

"I'll go with you if you like."

"I noticed from a distance your kindness

towards him. I believe you bound his foot with your own handkerchief."

"It was nothing," shrugged the Kapo. "He is an old man, after all. I was thinking of my father who is a musician in Weimar. If you would care to call upon him, I'll turn my battalion over to my assistant. You go right on in." And with that, he marched them off at a proper four-count, keeping in tune with the strains of the Horst Wessel Lied, which came from a distance in the compound.

I knocked at the door of twenty-eight, returning the smile of a uniformed orderly who was nearby.

"Come in," said a voice, which I recognized at once. Sure enough, it was someone I knew. He didn't recognize me.

"I see, old man, that you've injured your foot since I last saw you," I said, entering.

"I'm afraid I don't know you," said the older man, lying on his bunk. "Are you the one?"

"Which one?" I asked, drawing near.

"Come to take me to the retirement home. Here is my pink card."

"I see you've lost some weight this past year or two."

"I've not been eating well. But you see, I am

the first, today. I'm ready when you are. Here is my pink card. See! 118700! The same as here," he averred, rolling up his sleeve to show me a tattoo on his forearm. "The Kapo said to be first is an honor. Please, remember that when the time comes."

"I assure you, old man, I'm not here to take you to a retirement home, but rather to inspect the plumbing," I answered, trying to catch his eye.

"That's what they always say. They have to say that to fool the others on the compound. If the others knew that blockhouse twenty-eight was to be filled with those being permanently retired, there'd be a riot. . . . Everyone wants to retire, of course. Even though the wages are good. You can't fool me with your plumbing business. I've a pink card, see!"

"And will there be others with a pink card?"

"To be sure. But, you'll remember when it comes time to leave, that I was first. Promise me."

"You don't remember me at all? I am Rudin. You sold me that jewel. I paid you a goodly price."

"I don't know of what you speak. You just said you were a plumber. And now you're a man of jewels. Why must there always be these jokes? The other day when I asked the Kapo why we weren't being provided with toilet paper anymore, he said it was because the political writers in barracks twenty-nine were using it for propaganda and the Commandant had forbidden all paper for a month. Why don't they stick to their business instead of causing such a stink at Auschwitz. These political writers. Some are born fools, no matter what anyone says. They've said some awful things. It's a wonder the Commandant didn't put them on bread and water. Give one of those writers paper and they'll upset the applecart. Before you know it, they'll want to do away with the retirement home. I say the Commandant is crazy."

"While I'm waiting for the Kapo, may I inspect the plumbing?"

"I know you're making a joke. I knew it would be like this the day of departure. Jests from everybody. The only one with kindness in the whole battalion is the Kapo. You'll see. He kneeled and bound my foot with his own handkerchief. I know you're not here to check the plumbing, but to test me. Why you're the man from the pay office. You're seeking a bribe before you give me my pay chit. I asked the Kapo if he would have it converted into marks. He said they would do that at the retirement home; the pink card was a carte blanche to whatever I needed." And with this, the

Kapo came in, panting somewhat from his march, returning the smile of the uniformed orderly who was rummaging in the corner.

"Ah," said the Kapo, "did you reestablish your friendship? Have you been courteous, old man, with the man from the Commission of Inquiry?"

The older man grinned a toothless grin which spoke more than words, as much as to say that the Kapo was playing him a trick and he could see through it.

"I've brought your pay chit," said the Kapo, smiling in return. "You have seventeen hundred marks due. They'll take care of it for you as soon as you arrive. You'll see. Just show them the pink card."

The old man broke into tears. Unable to say more, he turned away and began to weep.

"It's all right, old man, have yourself a good cry," said the Kapo. Then turning to myself: "You see how cruel men can be. The men of his regular barracks have been chiding him since yesterday, knowing that he had received a pink card. They always do that, hardened as some of them are, despite daily lectures by our staff. They tease those who are to be retired."

"I see," I said, and made a note of it. "Why should they torment an old man? What do they tease him with?"

"Really, it's too crude. Come, if you've finished here, let's walk a bit. I'd enjoy showing you around, if you'd care to. No need of upsetting the old man further. There'll be others coming in here soon. Ten from my own battalion, but they insisted on working until noon. They'll be punched out then. Their last day, they get time and a half, and those few extra marks mean a great deal in retirement."

"But what do they tease them with?" I insisted.

The Kapo gave me a sign not to press, touching his fingers to his lips, pointing to the older man who had dozed off from fatigue, and beginning a tiptoe to the barracks door, he motioned me to follow, speaking quietly to the other uniformed orderly coming in, "Perhaps he'd better have a mild sedative, doctor. They've needled him badly."

Once outside the door, the Kapo went on, as he took me by the arm:

"The others have been teasing him until his nerves are nearly shattered. That's why he's put in a special barracks, as the others to retire will be. They reach a breaking point."

"Goodness," I asked, as he steered me on a walk in the direction of some warehouses at the far end of the compound, "what were they teasing him with that made him so upset? He thought I was the paymaster seeking a bribe out of his pay chit."

"That's one of the things they say, that before you retire they'll skin you of everything. Give me your dish, old man, one of them will say, you'll have a gold plate soon to eat off of; or, I can use your shoes, old man, since you'll soon be walking on air. They even try to make them believe that there's no such thing as retirement pay. You saw me give him his pay chit, did you not? We keep accurate records. By the way, I've taken a liking to you. I hope you don't mind my familiarity. Do you suppose your party might be staying the night? I'd like you to be my guest after you've had dinner with the Commandant."

"That's most kind and thoughtful, dear friend, but I'm afraid we must leave this evening. Our singer has a concert tomorrow evening and our casket maker, I believe, has a funeral at noon; the stone carver has a commission to fulfill. He's very upset over having had to leave not quite finished that which he considers will be his masterpiece, a figure of an angel, with childlike face, cut of a choice piece of Cararra marble, with the inscription, "In God We Trust," carved in script, a most delicate operation, as he has explained it. In ordinary print it would be simple. In script, the slightest jarring of the letters can turn it into quite another thing, as "The Devil is Upon Us." The Chairman of our Commission promised all of them that we'd leave by seven tonight, and if such were not the case, I would have been most delighted to spend the evening in your company."

"I hope that I might change your mind. Perhaps, then, this afternoon, after the surprise, before dinner, we might have a glass of wine."

"I'd enjoy that very much. But this surprise of which you speak?"

"Ah. The Commandant has sworn us to secrecy."

"That's quite unfair, you know, on such a grey day, with plumbing to inspect, to hint at such a matter," I responded.

"I assure you, it will be a pleasant one. Please, give it no further thought. Let's walk to the warehouses and I'll show you some of our operation.

About the old man, I did really appreciate your understanding of my asking you to refrain from upsetting him more."

"The old man appeared to have a semitic countenance, of one of the ancient races of man. Could that have had anything to do with the teasing of him?"

"Decidedly," said the Kapo. "Our Commandant does give them preferential treatment; men, women and children, and this has created a problem to which he has addressed himself."

"In short," I said, "your charges then do harbor feelings of anti-semitism." .

"They do. And, of course, it has created some difficulty. The Commandant often picks others for retirement to allay suspicions that he favors only those of semitic origin. This helps put a stop to the grumbles. Where, at first, they were favored with easier retirement as well as the more sought after positions that pay double time, the Commandant now insists that there be strict adherence to seniority. The Commandant has been scrupulously fair with your own countrymen, and more than generous with your slavic first cousins, even though we're at war with them."

"What does your workforce number now, dear Kapo?"

"Yesterday's count was 13,129. We have new arrivals coming in today. Four trains, I believe. Thus, you see, we must retire a number equivalent to a certain percentage of those who will arrive. We are understaffed, as it is. And, in the past several weeks, we've had not a few supply trains derailed enroute, creating a shortage of food. As you may have noticed, some of our workforce have lost weight as a result. There are some, of course, who bring it upon themselves. I, as you can see, am due for a diet, having gained some weight these past months, even though I exercise diligently."

"By the way, I meant to ask the name of that old man. I was sure I knew him, and yet, I'm not sure that I did. I'd like to call upon his family when I return to Warsaw. They'll be happy to know he is retiring and that the rumors were quite untrue."

"His name is 118700."

"Surely, you are joking. I mean his given name, as Sam, or Harry, or Adolf."

"We found the names created confusion and that some were cheating others of their just reward for labor done or not done. For example, we might at any one time have had seventy-five Otto Schmidts, and even though most middle initials might be different, they would exchange ration cards, work cards, hour cards, and yes, even the much sought after pink card. We've quite eliminated this confusion. An indelible imprint upon the forearm, and the matter is settled. The tattoo is quite painless; the custom is old. Hardly a sailor has failed to have the name of his favorite girl in a particular port of call tattooed upon his bicep, and indeed, as often, her shapely form, which did his bidding as he exercised his muscles. Most of our charges being landsmen of one kind or another, the tattoo almost becomes a symbol of rank, of place, for one can imagine himself a seafarer on a voyage of self-discovery. And, then, too, abolishing the name system has made it easier for those who have something to hide. Some men are, as you know, ashamed of their names. It carries a blemish. We have not a few here who have at one time or another embezzled from their employers, or employers who have embezzled from the government. They begin then with a clean slate, as it were. One can, upon retirement select any name he chooses. If he wishes, of course, he is quite free to use his own. We don't object one bit, in fact, we encourage it, for when useful service has been completed, one can take up his name with a new bearing and dignity, no matter how tarnished it might once have been. Such, you see, is the value of numbers. It has often happened that some have refused to go back to their names, having found with use that the number suited their character, or that friends had come to associate them with the diminutive of the whole. We had one man with six cights in his name. His comrades began calling him *six-huit*. A pleasant sounding name, is it not, especially when his given name had been Jacques. Ah, the French. Even though we're at war with them, I admire their gallic humor. But how political they are! The tradition of the revolution is in their bones. Even here, where independent trade unions are not quite in order, the compound belonging to a syndicate of the whole, they attempted to create a fraction of their own to work for portal to portal pay. Imagine! Payment while one is on his way to work, and payment on his way home! Who would be able to police such nonsense, if one stopped off enroute for a glass of beer in the local pub? Anticipating the possibility of the idea gripping the masses, as it were, the Commandant quickly issued an order forbidding pubs of any kind. So you see, the French proved to be their own worst enemies."

"And what building is this, dear Kapo?" I enquired of my guide, as we approached one of the many warehouses at the far end of the compound.

"This is storage warehouse number seven, if you'd care to have a look," as he guided me towards the door. "There are, in all, thirty-five."

"Dear Kapo," as he held the door for me to enter, "I must apologize for my mathematics. It has always been one of my poorer talents. But if my hearing has not failed me, I believe I understood you to say that you had 13,129 in your workforce by the last count. It would seem, then, that you count by tens. As I recall, the number tattooed on the old man's forearm—the one about to retire—was 118,700. Your latecomers would then be registered in the one hundred thirty thousands, if my rapid but unsure calculations are correct."

"That's it precisely. A single digit hardly seemed appropriate. It would have been demoralizing in the extreme. You do very well with figures, dear sir. The Commandant will be more than pleased with your acumen," smiled the Kapo.

"But, if I may correct you, I don't believe you have allowed for those who have retired, and we have been somewhat more liberal in this regard than other similar establishments. Our Commandant had to carry his ideas on such matters to the highest quarters, finally inducing those in command that a liberal retirement policy would be necessary to increase production, just as conversely an increase in production would automatically bring about more liberal retirement. Such are the dialectics of mathematics. Not having accounted for our liberal retirement plan, then, you have, quite correctly, in counting by tens, reached a number in the one hundred thirty thousands, and by the count I had already given you of 13,129 you would be correct. But we are already issuing names in the two million category; if I'm not mistaken, those arriving today being issued numbers in the higher divisions of the one million, four hundred thousand bracket. This, as you can readily calculate, by a simple mathematical equation, would give you the figure on hand—the number entering from the outset multiplied by ten, less the number retiring multiplied by ten, with some account being given to the number entering and retiring on the same day. On certain days, however, when saboteurs are at work derailing trains, the latter number will exceed the former by a considerable count. Thus, you see how heartless these pseudo-patriots are who destroy proper rail communications. By their acts of barbarism, they only increase the work load per man of those not retired, thus belying their expressed ideals, in truth, no more than propaganda designed to delude honest patriots. Our appeals to their good sense in the matter have failed, thus the Commissions of Inquiry, to bring to light the truth about our administration; and although yours is limited in jurisdiction to sanitation, others that follow will shed light on other matters."

"I see," I answered. "It is not too difficult mathematically when one works in multiples of ten. . . . Your warehouse number seven is well stocked with men's clothing. It would appear, at first glance, although we often allow our imaginations to soar when calculating quantities, that you have suits enough here for a substantial portion of Warsaw's population. These, then, presumably are sent by charitable enterprises from over Europe to clothe your indigent warders."

"Your perception is keen," smiled my Kapo guide. "I intend to speak at some length to the

Commandant, for, if I may say so, sir, without any reflection on those who selected the members of your Commission of Inquiry, it would seem to me as though they had not selected the most qualified person as Chairman. With all due respect. . . ."

"Tut, tut. You flatter me," I insisted. "I am not in politics at all and know little enough of sanitation as it is. But then. . . ."

"Nonsense," the Kapo insisted. "I do most seriously intend to express myself, off the record of course, to the Commandant on the subject. It seemed to me that the portly gentleman who is the Chairman looked a mite dull-witted, if I might use the expression. He seemed to be looking down, as though he were hardly interested in what was going on around or above him. I believe that the Chairman of any Commission should carry himself with a bearing commensurate with his rank."

"Hmm, well," I responded, "it is possible that you caught him, as the saying goes, when he wasn't looking. He is of a reflective bent by nature, and being a professor of languages, he may have, at that particular moment, been cogitating over a theory presently being espoused to the effect that Attila the Hun had spent a not inconsiderable length of time in this area, certain similarities between rare expressions sometimes heard in peasant households with those used in his day having been noted, and although such expressions are archaic to the world at large, they are, as I say, sometimes heard today, pronunciation differences notwithstanding."

"Ah," remarked the Kapo. "Attila! Yes! Our Commandant's findings in random excavating should prove most interesting to your Chairman then. You will recall the boot and my indicating that there lay a tale. . . ."

"We digress, I fear," I responded, anxious to get on with the routine matter of inspection. "Does this warehouse number seven hold all of the clothing sent by charitable enterprises?"

"Not at all, dear sir. In this warehouse, there are only suits for men, and not even all of those are here. The response to our appeal has been so great that we have been, to put it mildly, inundated. Warehouses number seven through twelve hold men's clothing. Altogether, by the last count, there were 319,297 suits. There were some 627,184 women's dresses, along with those undergarments, if you will excuse me, which go to complete a full wardrobe; some, of course, more delicate than others, some indeed, by the fine lace (forgive me, sir) which is the ultimate mark of a woman's dress, the exquisite embroidered detail, directly traceable to the finest shops of Paris. We can, if you choose, wander through warehouses eleven to sixteen. I could (I trust you implicitly) select some dainty negligee, all silk, hand stitched, if you've found such things hard to come by. Perhaps, one of your lady friends in Warsaw might appreciate your thoughtfulness. This has been an unusually bitter winter. . . ."

"I do appreciate your kind thought, my dear Kapo, but I don't believe it would be quite appropriate under the circumstances. To deprive even one of your warders of a single item of clothing proffered by the generous of heart from across the continent would be a betrayal of trust. . . . I see that the suits are cleaned and pressed, ready for wear."

"Yes. We do our own. It's cheaper that way. The steam generated in our plant is thus put to use. As you know, in modern synthetics, much fuel is consumed. Although we have been working on methods of increasing production per cubic foot of fuel consumed (our production has nearly doubled during the past four months) we have not yet found all of the answers. But, with the by-produced steam thus used for dry cleaning, we have cut our energy loss to a minimum."

"Presumably, then, these are issued after the Saturday night bath, so that your warders may attend Sunday mass in proper dress and entertain their weekly visitors?"

"Precisely so! Ah, if only the world could see as readily as yourself! How often have I heard the Commandant rail at dinner about our poor public relations, especially when rumors are circulating about the countryside which are shameless lies, formed of half-truths. You, sir, are witness to one as you stand in warehouse seven. You see a warehouse full of men's suits. As I've explained, there are twenty warehouses in all for clothing alone. If then, we didn't send clothing out by train, we would, as you can readily see, have to convert our warders quarters into clothing storehouses, condemning them to the outdoors and a certain cold death. We have even set up an agency for the express purpose of guaranteeing that all profits from clothing sold go to the children's fund. You have no idea how many reputable merchants—if you please, men willing to traffic in human misery would be a more apt title for them—have beseeched the Commandant to permit them to handle the sale as brokers. Many have even gone so far as to set up commission houses nearby for the purpose. And, as always, in time of war, black market and profiteering operations have plagued us. There have been not a few manufacturing establishments which have been pressing for special building considerations within walking distance in order that they might make use of any excess labor, free of charge. And not a few, under the circumstances of the shortage of manpower, have been contracted out by the day, their wages and hours protected by the syndicate of the whole, of which the Commandant is the honorary and acting president. Thus, we have held exploitation to a minimum. . . .But, to get back to the lie, if I may, that monstrous lie which has circulated to the effect that the clothes sent from Auschwitz by the trainload were the personal belongings of warders who had retired . . . how did it begin? An engineer, now serving twenty years for sedition, had told a friend that he had carried a trainload of clothing from Auschwitz to Warsaw. He told the truth as far as he went. The friend, to whom he had related the fact, related it to another, who, in turn, embellished upon it, until it was common gossip in the cafes of Europe. You are witness to the falseness of the lie. The clothing is here. You see it for your-self. Would you care to count the suits? What, pray, would we do if we didn't ship carloads of it out on outgoing trains? Our initial appeal made such an impress upon those who heard it that it seems they all shed their clothes at once. Here, let me show you warehouse five. You will have to see it to believe it; how those who are asked for things have responded with such generosity. Here, this door leads to number five. Look at them! Pros-thetics! Hundreds, if not thousands! Artificial limbs of every possible description. These would fit a child of ten. And, look at this fine arm, sir! What would you say of its donor? Do you like guessing games? From an old pensioner, perhaps, who heard our appeal? I would say, from its shape and size, the man was small of frame. From the contour of the shoulder, that he was hollow chested, plagued by a wracking cough! Yet, patriotic enough to loan his good right arm—give, yes, for surely he would not expect it back in time of war. Although so generous a patriot might never see the front and achieve that glory which only the battlefield can give, he was, nonetheless, a hero of the first rank. . . .And, look at this pair of legs! You can see this man, can't you, as the enemy retreats from his village, climbing slowly to his rooftop, despite a plea from an invalid wife, and with an arm as strong, if not stronger than yours or mine, whipping a grenade into a retreating column. . . . And now, without these limbs, the column would retreat unscathed. . . ."

"My dear Kapo, you have a poet's imagination, coupled with a worthy patriotism. I would venture a guess that you keep a daily journal of your observations, planning a serious novel when the war is over. Or do you already have work in progress, modest about having it read? I see you are blushing! As you offered me a choice negligee for a friend, from your many storehouses, allow me to return your thoughtfulness by suggesting that I have a friend, who has many friends in the publishing world, who is constantly on the look-out for aspiring writers, whom I might persuade, at her usual fee, to judge your efforts. I should, however, in all fairness, indicate to you that it is best to avoid political matter, not for the lack of demand, but because there is little market for it in our troubled times; and although I am loathe to give you professional advice, should you touch upon erotic or sensual matter, I would suggest, if you are serious, the utmost restraint, for where it might seem there is no demand for it, there is, at all the better houses for which she solicits, an insistence upon delicate handling of so decisive a subject, a contribution, as it were, to the efforts to achieve a just and a lasting peace. You are blushing! Ah, you do have a manuscript! Seriously, my dear Kapo, I would be more than happy."

"Oh, really, sir. I'm afraid I don't have anything finished. I've dabbled now and then, but little more. I hardly begin when I've come to an end. It seems that I can't carry a plot. Oh, how I've hoped that I might be fated to write The Novel about the war, a work that would be definitive, that would stand alone as a work of art, for its own sake, only to find that before I've sketched a single character or shaped my story, I'm caught in a web of hallucinations from which I find it almost impossible to extricate myself. I am subject to nightmares. . . . If you could intercede for me with the Commandant. I've asked for duty at the front to no avail. If I could have seen with my own eyes those great battles that have shaped the destiny of nations for centuries to come; had I been able to see, with my own eyes, the heroism of millions as our great armies liberated country after country; had I, in short, been anything but what I am, fated to live out these years behind the lines, as it were, it might have been another story. My work is weary, flat, stale, unprofitable, reflecting an ennui of the soul, which I try to make myself believe does not exist, but what one says consciously cannot alter a given situation in terms of its inmost reality. Don't you agree? When one is where little of import happens, one's work will lack in incident, action, even thought, and one's characters, no matter what the author's imaginative powers might be, no matter how much he might be able to assimilate experience vicariously, are not whole. In short, when nothing happens which can kindle one's imagination. . . ."

"By the way, dear Kapo, it seems that the chimneys at Birkenau are smoking fiercely, as though the Devil himself, at this very moment, were burning a thousand Fausts engraved on oil parchment."

"Yes. They do have a full head of steam. I take it you were jesting, then, about a publisher."

"Indeed not," I replied. "Really, my dear Kapo, one mustn't be so modest about his work. One must believe in himself. Every beginning writer must pass through that ordeal by fire, even though one might feel as though his very soul were being consumed and then made light of, gone up in smoke, as it were. He is, of course, baring his soul to that first reader. Once out of his hands, the possession of another, the first page open to another's eyes and all seems lost. He suffers a thousandfold more than in the writing. Indeed, he's ready to accuse that first reader of prying, and before a dozen pages have been scanned, he is crying murder, praying for its return."

"Would you, then, condescend to read my work . . . seriously?"

"I'd consider it a privilege."

"It isn't much. . . . As I say, I've only dabbled. But if you could read it, sir; if you could tell me whether it is good or not, good enough to really take myself seriously, I would then request again, nay, demand, a change of duty, the eastern front, to be specific. If it were possible . . . to write The Novel . . . that could stand alone . . . for all time. You seem a man of culture. You can understand what it means, then, to be haunted by the fear that one is fated to live out a dreary existence here, while elsewhere, history is being made. Fate has been kinder to some. To be haunted, yes, by the knowledge that someone, somewhere, has his pen in hand, creating that same work which has been, so to speak, shaping itself. . . ."

"You overwhelm me, my dear Kapo. I meant it most sincerely. Why don't you put your manuscript in the limousine before I leave, or you could, if you choose, mail it to me. My card. The address is there. There were, before we departed Warsaw, cannonlike rumbles in the distance, rapidly approaching from the east; and should one of their shells, God forbid, strike a direct hit, you might then send it to me at the Red Cross in Geneva."

"You are most sincere and kind, dear sir. How unlike the usual run of people I've known here at Auschwitz. Each of them with his own petty axe to grind, concerned more with his worldly place than with that which elevates him above the crowd. How few such people there are left at Auschwitz! . . . There, before you is warehouse number one. As you can see, it is padlocked. Your reputation as a jeweler's merchant preceded you, of course. I never dreamed that it would be my good fortune to be able to accompany you on a tour of inspection. To have come to know a man of culture as yourself was beyond my fondest expectations, and as your Chairman may have informed you, the Commandant was reserving the singular honor of touring Birkenau to that member of the Commission who proved the most worthy. I trust that you will permit me to make my sincerest feelings known to him before the tour of inspection is completed."

"Come, come, my dear Kapo. You flatter me, I assure you. Although I carry the title, jeweler's merchant, I am, in truth, little more than a petit-bourgeois tradesman. In fact, little more than a shopkeeper of sorts. If such esteem is to be bestowed upon any member of the Commission, I would call your attention to this fact, most of all. . . . And yet, I would consider it an honor to visit Birkenau. I have devoted much study, such as a layman is capable of naturally, to the composition of matter, both organic and inorganic, and their being decomposed, as it were, to their basic elements. I see that your warehouse number one contains a substantial shipment of gold, the basic reserves of all stable governments, brought directly from your central banking system to be melted down into lasting crowns and half crowns by your professors of dentistry!"

"Ah, your ability to perceive is beyond my comprehension. Here, you see gold ingots, yes, shipped under armed guard across a thousand miles of partisan infested country for the teeth of our warders. There, in those boxes, you see the half-crowns, crowns and tidbits of dental cutlery, shaped by our technicians' finest skills, ready for insertion into any ailing tooth. Our dental staff does not believe in extractions (oh, how quick some dentists are to want to yank a sterling molar) and even when there are abscesses, the Commandant must give his own approval to the removal of a tooth; this, only after the most elaborate root canal work has been done. If you'd care to, I could arrange an afternoon dental appointment for you. Perhaps you've found gold hard to come by in Warsaw. Please, I do insist you accept, since you were reluctant to allow me to present you with an undergarment. Our technicians are known for their painless dentistry."

"How kind, my dear Kapo. Permit me, if you will, to take a raincheck on it. I might, some week-end, in the not too distant future, motor down with a second cousin who cannot abide the needle, his dentist insisting there is no gas to be had in all of Warsaw."

You'd like to use the telephone? Your office? By all means, cher ami. We've come a long way since breakfast. I'll sun myself right here on this bench and converse with your Harbor Lady. I promise you I won't leave while you're gone.

My address? Not far from your own. We can see the jewel this evening, yes. You're smiling. You don't believe there is a jewel. It's not that at all? You didn't know you were smiling? It couldn't be an abscessed molar? There is an ancient remedy for neuralgia, known to have been used by the Shah of Persia in the twelfth century, a mild hashish without addictive effects. As you wish. I hope an aspirin will give you relief. Yes, I'll wait for you here.

CHAPTER VIII

You finished your calls? The exchange, I gather, is in a flurry of trading. Please, I beg of you, cher ami, not to let me keep you from your profession. You do, after all, have obligations. The pigeons, yes.

> A lost dove stopped upon a fountain wall
>   and spoke to me of us.
> She knew that I was lonely and gave me peanuts
>   that Paris lovers had shared with her.

Those lines? An unknown poet of sorts I met in the Tuileries Garden in Paris. A wanderer who sat by the hour penning epigrammatic letters to his loved ones, who had been lost somewhere in Europe during the era of voluntary labor. He had trained pigeons not only to eat from his hand but to home for him as well, carrying his pleas to the remotest corners of the continent, believing that one of his letters would soon be answered. The authorities put a stop to it, of course, insisting that he have a license, but alas, such licenses had not been issued for half a century. Undismayed by his temporary retreat, he has taken up residence in your fair city as a flower vendor. I learned this morning that he had moved to a busier location uptown, not for more lucrative trade, but for the greater number of people who will pass by, his wife and daughter both being fond of roses.

The Commission of Inquiry? The surprise? That had to do with the scaffold which carpenters had been assembling since our arrival. You will recall that an investigation had been underway in blockhouse thirty since morning. Someone had been found murdered in his bed. And, despite a general opinion quite anxiously expressed by the deceased's own colleagues in number thirty that he had taken his own life, they were not believed.

A thorough examination throughout the greater part of the day, conducted as I later learned from one of the members of the Commission, with zeal and determination by those in charge, photographs taken of the position in which he was found, the number of wrinkles in his sackcloth blanket counted, the contour of the impression made upon his pillow cast in plaster, a thirty inch shoestring not matching the color of his shoes which could have been used as a garrote, clutched in his hand, and other incriminating evidence all pointing to a circumcised wretch four bunks away.

Although weighing no more than ninety-seven pounds, and it hardly seemed possible, upon initial observation, that so slight a framed man could do in someone twice his size, the prosecution, in the course of the trial, which, to be just in the matter, was conducted with all due consideration for procedure (the defendant having a court-appointed defense attorney—one of his colleagues in blockhouse thirty) cited Hugo's *Les Miserables* at great length to prove its point. Who would have thought that a man could scale a wall thirty feet in height, without a break in its surface? Not only had Jean Valjean performed such feats time and time again, but even during the bleakest period of his inhuman incarceration (one logically surmised that a century before the trial in time, French prisoners were ill-fed and ill-nourished) considerably under his regular weight, he had shown prodigious feats of strength which would have been discounted as the figment of a novelist's imagination, had there not been proof of those feats. Thus, the prosecution proved, conclusively, that the accused had left his bunk in the still of the night, scaled the wall to the ceiling, and thence had made his way, simian-like, the sixteen feet separating his own bed from the deceased's, and had, without lowering himself to the floor, suspended himself from the ceiling by his toes and had throttled his comrade with his bare hands, the pressure of the thumbs on the windpipe exerted with such instant and telling force that there were no visible markings on the flesh. He had then removed one of the shoestrings from the deceased's own shoes, performed the garrote with the victim's toothbrush.

If the court proceedings lasted through most of the day, the jury's deliberation (comprised of former colleagues) lasted less than an hour, the accused found guilty of murder in the first degree, sentenced to be hung at sunset on the very scaffold which had been in the process of construction since our arrival, the prosecution (not uncommon with prosecutors) sure of the case. By special order of the Commandant, it was decreed that everyone at Auschwitz would witness the execution.

At the appointed hour, the condemned was seated in an ancient tumbril (the Commandant had a love of antiques and had prevailed upon a friend situated near Paris to purloin the relic from a museum of the Revolution) and driven through the compound, the procession, headed by several Kapos, proceeding to the accompaniment of a hundred rolling drums. One of the thirteen thousand, mesmerized by the solemnity of the occasion—the procession, the drums, the tumbril, the condemned, with head shaven, eyes fallen, skin jaundiced—shouted for all to hear: "Off with his head! Long live the Republic!" which was echoed choruslike as the thirteen thousand surged forward, nearly crushing the procession before it reached its destination. Only the forcible intervention of a security force brought the procession safely to the scaffold, which the prisoner ascended, head high, accompanied by our priest.

When the rope was made fast—(the prisoner had refused a blindfold), the Commandant's eyes riveted upon that curling column of smoke rising majestically against a background of brilliant sunset (as only winter can give us), his hand poised, the eyes of the hangman trained upon that hand, waiting for the signal to trip the door, the drums pressing as the beat of the roll increased in tempo for what seemed like an eternity, the tension broken only by the inaudible fainting of our soprano (the Commandant's wife was standing at her side), the face of the condemned having taken on an indefinably sad but beatific expression, as though in that curling orange an outstretched hand had suddenly made its appearance, reaching across the two miles separating them to uplift his weary soul—the Commandant walked slowly over to the condemned (the hangman's jaw dropped perceptibly, and had it been anyone but the Commandant treading on that sacred ground in which he was God, his foot would have kicked the trip) and fastened his eyes upon those of the condemned, who raised his own to return the gaze. After what seemed an hour of tortuous agony, in reality no more than a few seconds, the Commandant removed the rope.

As suddenly, the drums ceased and thirteen thousand voices uttered a hoarse cry in unison.

Taking immediate advantage of the hypnotic effect his act of charity had had upon the multitude gathered below him, he read a brief proclamation of clemency—that reluctant as he was to countermand a decision of a justly constituted court of the accused's peers, he had, after long deliberation, decided upon a full pardon, knowing that the agony the prisoner will have suffered in the few moments just elapsed will bring about a proper cleansing of the conscience and regeneration of the soul. He then called upon everyone to bow his head for a moment of silence to find forgiveness and mercy in his heart that they might welcome their brother back into the family of man. Faint murmurs, beginning at the far side of the compound, becoming more audible, were silenced, as the Commandant raised his hand and cried out:

"He that is without sin among you, let him first cast a stone at him."

His admonition was met with silence. He went on:

"You have forgotten, sinners that you are. I ask you again, that whichever of you is without sin, let him first cast a stone at him." Again, silence. "Let us then bow our heads and recall the words of John, Chapter 8, Verse 9: 'And they which heard it, being convicted by their own conscience, went out one by one, beginning at the eldest, even unto the last.' "

As though the heavens above had at that moment opened, the smoke in the distance disappeared, the world, itself, had stopped turning, the thirteen thousand, with bowed heads, dispersed themselves to their blockhouses.

The Commandant turned to the young man, the condemned, saying, "Go now, and sin no more." As he descended the scaffold, assisted by our priest, the wife of the Commandant and our soprano wept over him.

All of the members of the Commission gathered at the foot of the scaffold, the Commandant, on descending, extended his personal invitation to be his guests at supper. Needless to say, none of us found words adequate to express our wonder and awe.

It wasn't until we were gathered in his quarters that I found enough courage to address him.

"Excellency. One does not easily find words with which to express his gratitude for the compassion shown at sunset."

"You may thank Dostoevsky, or the Czar, actually," he responded.

"How so?" I queried.

"I had previously known almost by heart Dostoevsky's *Crime and Punishment*," the Commandant went on, as we sipped wine (he mentioned in passing that he would not allow hard liquor to be imbibed on the premises and what he denied the establishment as a whole he exercised as a discipline upon his own household) "and to some extent his lengthy *Karamazov,* and had heard, as one often does, in a literary circle to which I had belonged in Westphalia, that the author himself had had his life spared by the Czar, after having been condemned to death, the sentence commuted to some years in exile in Siberia, but not until I chanced upon his *Idiot* quite recently, where this experience was conveyed by the princely Myshkin, did I fully realize what a traumatic experience it had been for Dostoevsky, and how the trauma had tapped, as it were, a hitherto hidden well in him, which was to overflow as though the well itself were ink and he but the agent who held pen in hand to write down what had been ordained. Not that I entertain hopes that the young man whose life was spared might blossom into another Dostoevsky, that would be more than a miracle, in truth, but he might go on to produce a poem or two, if not even a novel or a play, in which case, one would be more than grateful. But please, dear friends, let's make no more of the matter," he insisted, blushing the while. (I gathered, on observing him closely, that he was inwardly shy and most reluctant to speak either about himself, his fine deed of the afternoon, or of his accomplishments in general; in fact, was embarrassed.)

"May I then propose a toast, Excellency. To the Commandant, whose compassion has filled the cup of mercy to overflowing, who has, today, set an example for all of us, nay, for all of mankind, and especially those who are so placed by circumstances to have to pass judgment upon their fellow man. May he have long life."

"Thank you, and allow me," rejoined the Commandant, "to propose a toast to each of you who, as members of your Commission, will keep the flame of truth burning to cast light where before there was darkness, who will, for all of posterity, have set an example of self-sacrifice in the interests of history, as it is being made and unmade, in the service of the best interests of your country and the cause of liberation of humanity from earthly strife. May you be blessed with more than life."

"My dear Rudin," the Commandant continued, putting a Chopin Concerto on his victrola as the others of our party were being shown an assortment of antiques and anthropological specimens by our hostess. "I have learned so many excellent reports from one of our most learned Kapos about your insight into matters. I had hoped he might be with us this evening, but unfortunately, he and some of his colleagues suffered some slight mishap in our procession. He spoke in glowing terms of your ability to perceive the whole quickly when confronted with but a semblance of the whole."

"It is nothing, really, Excellency. My training, perhaps, as a jeweler's merchant may have given me an advantage in this regard; an ancient craft, in which one must be able to visualize the finished jewel from what might be no more than rough stone, as one must, from component parts create in his mind's eye a finished work."

"I trust that you did not misconstrue my use of the tumbril for the condemned as an idle theatrical gesture."

"Not at all, Excellency. I would say that you rescued the tumbril once and for all from a hitherto unjustified bloody association. More than one historian has repeated that silly rhyme: 'Who rides the tumbril to the guillotine, forever after loses his bean.' It was my good fortune not so long ago, while making a study of the famous necklace Marie Antoinette was wearing on the flight to Varennes, that I chanced upon a story by a distant cousin of the Marquis de Sade, in which he related how he had ridden the tumbril to the very foot of that monstrous device to be rescued by a personal order of Robespierre, the cousin of Sade's having been a childhood companion of the great revolutionary."

"Magnificent, my dear Rudin. Our best Kapo did not in his reports do you justice. That same obscure work of which you speak is one of the treasures of my library, and even if I had not been acquainted with Dostoevsky, I would have used the tumbril as I did, to restore it, as it were, to its proper place in our museums. Prior to today, whoever has seen a replica of it has shied away. How often have I seen parents, accompanied by their children at museums of the Revolution, point to it as though it were the Devil himself, and defame it as the carriage of death, that little known historical fact with which you acquainted yourself being known only to a few. And how deeply the idea about the tumbril has penetrated modern man's consciousness, you heard yourself this afternoon, when one of our more outspoken citizens, on seeing the condemned ride in it, even with the guillotine not present, shouted, 'Off with his head! Long live the Republic.' How much has this conveyance suffered at the hands of historians and novelists!"

"Our museumologists must be forever grateful to you, Excellency, as one day our historians must be to that distant cousin of the Marquis de Sade for having shed light not only upon the tumbril but upon Robespierre, himself, who, known to this obscure writer since childhood (they often having chased butterflies together) was not a cruel or a vengeful man at all; in fact, unhappy in the extreme, that history had selected him for a difficult task, by nature being warm-hearted, kind and of a mild disposition, loving his family dearly and wishing, in his innermost nature, to have been free to be a scrivener in some out of the way library, making some small contribution to lettres."

"You do then believe in fate and I am most delighted. Your insight into the inner logic of history is astounding. How correct you are about Robespierre! Just as the world will one day understand the inner nature of our own dear Führer, who picked up the mantle of revolution reluctantly, having cherished as a youngster an ardent desire to paint. I had the privilege of knowing him before he had achieved his pre-eminent position as leader of the civilized world. How often did he express the deepest chagrin that the art school to which he had applied did not recognize his earnest desire, even if in his early work he did not display the genius and aptitude for which he has since become so famous. Strong men are always torn between the desire to be a man of action or a withdrawn creator, and yet, the highest genius is that which combines the two. The artist who shapes his own world on canvas or paper, alas, must regret at times that he did not head great armies, make lesser nations greater, greater lesser, do away with man's earthly misery, in a new familial order. It grieves me, truly, dear Rudin, to see so intelligent and discerning a man as yourself a chain smoker, with so little regard for your health. You may have seen those signs situated in all of our latrines, forewarning against the injurious effects of cigarettes. Our medical staff has found conclusive evidence that their habitual use produces lung cancer. You will forgive me for intruding into what is your own private concern, however, I have been witness to the tragic fate of countless otherwise healthy men, about to be retired after completing their tour of duty, having earned by our records a substantial sum, more than sufficient to care for all of their physical needs forever after, stricken with this dread killer. Our educational campaigns on the matter have proved quite hopeless. We have had not a few, when informed they were so stricken, take their lives by charging our fence while the current is on. I had entertained hopes, when these glowing reports were first brought to me today, of your quickness to discern our Party's achievements, that you might be induced to remain with us here, become one of our staff, as it were. Although we have achieved a remarkable productive capacity and have been acclaimed in many quarters for our genius as organizers, our public relations have gone from bad to worse. And what, pray, can all of the organizational genius in the world do without a proper appreciation of it by the European community and nations abroad? I was quite prepared to enquire whether there were not a possibility of giving you the rank of major, in charge of all matters pertaining to our relations with the public at large."

"Excellency. . . ."

"You would have to give up cigarettes."

"Excellency, you are. . . ."

"You should know that our Fuhrer was once addicted with the habit, breaking it by sheer effort of will. One must believe enough in himself and his cause. One must know that he has a contribution to make, no matter how great or small, to the inevitable march of history. Each of us is, in truth, no more than a pawn in that march, ordained by the unified will of mankind. Why, I ask you, did the Americans intervene in a family quarrel? Because they are pragmatists, without any conception of historical necessity. They are brash and unwise in the extreme, incapable of separating illusion from reality. . . . If you will excuse me for a few moments, dear Rudin. My wife is beckoning. It is our children's bedtime, and then, I would upon returning, ask to be excused further to enquire of your Chairman's reaction to the report. You will think then upon the matter? You could try a pipe to begin with."

"Your offer is most generous, Excellency. I do most humbly apologize for my weakness as a human being. I am hardly worthy to have brought such signal attention to myself. I have had little experience in the techniques of advertising."

"Ah, think nothing of that. We would send you to school for a short course. But, first you would have to come to some conclusion about smoking. Think upon it for a week or two."

"Before you leave, if I may, Excellency, on behalf of the Kapo who was kind enough to conduct me through your storehouse. . . ."

"I know what you would ask, that he be relieved of his present duties to go to the front that he might collect impressions and material for a war novel. This matter has come up before. You should not consider me wanting in appreciation of art, in any form, and if you will forgive my immodesty, I have planned an assignment for the young man, having myself accumulated several notebooks, kept in the form of a daily journal, which I feel would be of value to the world; a modest biography. If you could, before you leave, suggest to him that a gesture, an offer, on his part, made willingly, rather than a request coming from myself, would be most graciously accepted. It would be more than unseeming, I'm afraid, to broach the matter myself."

"I would consider it an honor, Excellency."

"Until later, then. My wife beckons again. Come friends, one and all, be merry. I shall join you in a moment. Perhaps, the lovely lady will entertain you with a song. Do fill your glasses, gentlemen, and please, I beg you, let us not slight our concert singer." And with a courtly gesture, he kissed her hand as his wife shot him a curt glance from the doorway.

"How fare we, friends?" I enquired of our party, gathered about a rare anthropological specimen.

"The report leaves a matter quite undisposed," answered our Chairman, as he turned the pages.

"That portion of the compound that was declared out of bounds?" asked our casket-maker.

"It seems that every establishment has a skeleton in the closet," responded our Chairman, "yet I must express chagrin at the veiled threat that had been directed towards myself this morning."

"Each of us has a cross to bear," added the stonecarver. "I am inclined, without more ado, to sign the report, the undisclosed area not having been inspected notwithstanding. That portion of the compound more than likely has a separate septic tank. I have a commission to fulfill and would leave before we have supped."

"These heads, diminutive in size, must have once belonged to pygmies, although this first seems of an unusually scholarly mien," I suggested, pointing to a unique specimen adorning a table near the piano.

"They are not pygmy heads, though pygmy made, dear Rudin," responded our concert singer. "Our hostess was remarking upon them just before leaving to bid her children goodnight. These were sent her by the wife of another Commandant working near Weimar, whose father, it seems, has explored countless New Guinea jungles, coming upon these specimens of shrunken heads among not altogether savage pygmy tribes. You were right about the scholarly countenance, this head belonging to a colleague of her father who had disappeared on one of his explorations. Pygmies are not head hunters by tradition, but rather head shrinkers, out of a hidden compulsion to reduce all who wander into their domain to their own size. Quite a contrary opinion had heretofore been held by anthropologists. So explained our hostess."

"A most interesting scientific discovery which should prove of some value in years to come," I answered as the Commandant reappeared.

"Ah, dear friends, I hope we found our sanitation quite in order on your tour of inspection, and we can, this very evening, submit a report of our findings to our superiors, that rapid publication might quickly follow to scotch those rumors fabricated by an outlaw press," declared the Commandant amiably.

"Aside from the matter of that portion of the compound which was declared out of bounds, Excellency, there was the matter of the boot outside of barracks twenty-nine," I answered, on behalf of my colleagues.

"The boot outside of twenty-nine?" asked our Chairman.

"There lies a tale," responded the Commandant, "which the noble Rudin may soon enlarge upon, his extraordinary discerning powers a boon to our enterprise. The key, Rudin, is Yorick. Dwell upon it while we dismiss this other matter pertaining to that portion of the compound which has been declared 'off-limits.' My wife had hoped, dear lady, that you might sing a lullaby to our children, and we men might, in the interim, finish the business with dispatch. You are generous, indeed. Up the stairs and to your right. Now gentlemen. How shall we proceed? Yes, there was the matter of the area which I thought it best not be mentioned in the report, hence I took the liberty of suggesting that you forbear inspection of it, inasmuch as there is a woman member of your Commission. You will agree, gentlemen, that morality which is formal devours, exceeds itself, so to speak, and by virtue of its excess borders upon the immoral itself. All communities must strive for morality without which there would not be civilized life, and yet, that morality which restrains itself from becoming formalized has been achieved by sensible men everywhere only when recognizing human weakness. Life would indeed be quite unbearable if people were asked to thwart nature, even though the more ascetic of us might extend ourselves to the limits of endurance. I am sure our reverend father understands this better than those of us who have not been chosen for so noble a calling—the demands of celibacy, the few capable of achieving it for any length of time, how unwise to require it of anyone incapable of such physical and mental discipline, experience showing that they soon jump off the deep end, if you will forgive my use of the vernacular. Knowing beforehand that there was a lady member of the Commission, I took the liberty, gentlemen. It was in deference to her sensibilities. Then, too, there might have been a misconstruction of intent and purpose."

"She is intelligent, Excellency," broke in our casket-maker. "A magnificent voice, as well."

"Yes, a noble woman," added the priest.

"Gentlemen, I pray you," pleaded the Commandant. "I did not intend any reflection upon the beautiful lady, either individually or as a member of the Commission. We have considered ourselves honored to the highest degree and it was for this reason alone that I took the liberty."

"She spoke with awe and reverence of yourself, Excellency," added our Chairman. "Your act of clemency. . . ."

"I am more than honored, believe me. What would you have me do? The world-wide movement for women's rights, now nearly a century old, has so penetrated the consciousness of women and has become so sweeping in its demands that one is hard put, in time of war, to strike a balance between what is proper and improper. Our citizens have dubbed the area 'the nunnery.' But on a visit paid us, some months ago, by the Commandant of Buchenwald and his wife, the latter, in conjunction with my own, threatened to carry the matter over my head. Their righteous indignation was not un-expected and commendable, indeed, just. In fact, gentlemen, they were so enraged that they wrote a letter without my knowledge to the Party press accusing our administration of trafficking in white slavery. Fortunately, the editor is an old friend and brought it to my attention before printing it. You may well imagine what would have come of our appeals for clothing and other necessities, to which there has been so overwhelming a response. As much as I sympathized with their feelings, engen-dered by virtue of birth into what was once the weaker sex, as well as their social indignation, we have been faced with the problem of officers and guards, separated by the fortunes of war from their wives and loved ones, and although they are required upon admission to our select corps to take vows, unfortunately, they do not include celibacy."

"It seems . . . " began our Chairman.

"I understand your concern, dear Chairman. I ask, too, of yourself, forbearance for the unfortunate remarks directed towards yourself upon arrival by an over-zealous Colonel, recently promoted, brash as a result, indulging in his new found authority to the point of crudity. He was demoted shortly thereafter, I assure you. I can only regret that my former assistant, a man of charm and wit, could not have been here to receive you. He was called to more pressing duties at the front. I would ask, in conclusion, gentlemen, that you put yourselves in my place. It is not easy to be a Commandant. Where all might, at first glance, appear as sugar and spice, I assure you there is brimstone and sulphur."

"A question, if I may, Excellency," I intruded here, on behalf of my colleagues, who were exchanging thought and opinion upon the matter before them. "I trust that the vows taken for the nunnery are voluntary, and that they are permitted to retire."

"Most assuredly, dear Rudin. In fact, I neglected to add that as a concession to the wife of the Commandant at Buchenwald, somewhat more outspoken than my own on the matter, we altered our retirement policy, increasing the proportion of women in relation to men. Ah, I see our gracious lady has returned. Gentlemen, more wine, and do, I implore you, partake of our buffet supper while your Chairman and I finish the business at hand. Perhaps, dear Rudin, you will be kind enough to assist your Chairman to cross a T or two, dot an I, in the fine print. Come, tell me whether you have solved the riddle of the boot in front of barracks twenty-nine; or do you shy away from riddles?"

"Excellency, I am reminded of Oedipus, who, in solving that riddle which had plagued ancient Thebes, the myth surrounding the Sphinx being of such a nature that the Gods themselves cursed him for it, and fearing that I tread on what may be holy ground, I thought it might be best. . . ."

"Come, come, dear Rudin. You are not of a superstitious bent! Perhaps the clue was insufficient?"

"A boot may be a tail, if one were upended,

as a boot may tell a tale, if it is a telltale boot. To twist the lion's tail would make him roar."

"But what of Yorick?"

"It was the clue that led me to recall a now obscure tale, as it did to draw upon our Chairman's versatility with languages, both living and dead, and the remarkable coincidence of the translation of Auschwitz to Eronisle, which, with Yorick, led me to find in Eronisle the name of Elsinore (in ancient times more of our languages were writ from right to left) which then places the grave-digger scene of Hamlet in this region, rather than Denmark, as we are told; Denmark used by the dramatist as a mask, of course, and the gravedigger scene not, as so many have thought, a comic epi-sode designed to break the tension of the tragedy, but rather a clue to what he had discovered in this unknown master's tale, found recently in Warwick castle, not far from Stratford that at Eronisle, Attila had had countless tens of thousands dig their own graves before they were put to death. This writer's tale dates from the time of the Crusades, which is why the dramatist selected a tale for his gravedigger's scene which dated from the twelfth century. Thus, the peasant saying, 'Life Was Avoided Here For a Thousand Years, While Death

Kept Watch.' It is hardly coincidence that Shakespeare's use of words throughout the play as 'dank, weed, rotten, rank,' corroborated what this same obscure Crusader had related about the region of Eronisle. This should shed some light on that question which so many Shakespearean scholars have written tomes about, whether he had or had not been outside of England, his remarkable grasp of the character of place and people reflecting first hand observation, whether in *The Taming of the Shrew* referring to Lombardy as the 'pleasant garden of Italy' (which we know it is) or referring to the citizens of Pisa as 'grave' (which surely no one would dispute); or his uncanny sense of a storm at sea in *The Tempest,* or his gravedigger's scene at Eronisle. I would have it that he had traveled widely, despite his ability to make use of otherwise little known works which had preceded him."

"Magnificent, dear Rudin. I have a copy of that Warwick manuscript to which you refer in my library, treasured as highly as that rare work on Robespierre. It was the boot that led me back to the manuscript, which, in turn, led me to explore the countryside hereabout, and this is, indeed, the Eronisle of *Hamlet*."

"Nature, it seems," I went on, "played a rude

trick upon Attila. Those countless thousands buried in mass graves, covered hurriedly with quicklime to disintegrate them (history has it that he was retreating before a superior force converging from east and west and wished to leave no traces) were preserved by this same quicklime, which, mixing with the naturally acid soil, produced an opposite effect."

"You have put the noble Oedipus to shame," averred the Commandant.

"I hope the Gods will not be angry," I answered, as our Chairman finished reading the report. "Excellency, you pale. . . ."

"It is nothing," smiled the Commandant, "a chill caught upon the scaffold. The winters here are severe. I trust," he went on, directing his remarks to the Chairman, "that the report is sufficiently studied and that you will have your colleagues sign it before leaving. I would a word with my wife. And, dear Rudin," he went on, turning back to myself, "I'd prefer that you remain with us here at Auschwitz after your colleagues leave that we might confer about the matter of your joining our staff."

"Excellency, I have an early morning appointment with our Lord Mayor, who is planning a ball for members of your general staff quartered in our vicinity, a victory celebration, I believe. I have designed a coronet," I answered.

"We can, within the hour, reach the Lord Mayor by telephone, but should the lines be out of use for reasons of security, I'm sure the Chairman would, upon his arrival in the morning, be most willing to convey to him your regrets. My wife beckons again. You will excuse me," as our casket-maker hastened to where the Chairman and myself stood.

"I'm told our chauffeur is waiting for us," he volunteered cheerily. "Can we finish our business here with dispatch. I've an early morning funeral to prepare for."

"What say you of the nunnery?" enquired our Chairman. "I believe the sanitation elsewhere is quite in order."

"We must include the nunnery," chided our priest, as he and the other two members of our Commission approached.

"What is the nunnery?" asked our concert singer.

"A nunnery is where nuns live," quoth the stonecarver.

"The Commandant would have Rudin remain," reported our Chairman.

"Would you remain, Rudin? Is it your choice?" asked the casket-maker.

"The Commandant requested it," answered our Chairman. "It seems that Rudin has an insight into riddles."

"If it's against his will, I say we must protest," answered our concert singer.

"There's the matter of the nunnery," responded our priest.

"The Commandant waits upon the report," answered the Chairman. "We might recall, reverend father, his admonition about formal morality."

"The Commandant grows pale," said the stonecarver. "Is there room for compromise? The nunnery for Rudin?"

"The Commandant was about to sit himself at table," I conjectured, as I stole a fleeting glance across the room where he was shouting at his wife.

"Who has done this to me?" he enquired of her angrily.

"Come, you've not supped, dear husband. It has been a trying day. It is your nerves alone that fray. The world is as it is yet," she answered as she led him to his chair.

"I say, who has done this to me?" he repeated, thrusting her arm away.

"Please, we have guests, dear husband," she chided.

"The boot outside of twenty-nine. Who dug the boot and placed it in my chair?" he shouted for all to hear. "Away, I say. Take the boot away or else he'll rue the day."

"It is nought but your fancy, dearest husband. The boot is yet at twenty-nine. I saw it myself this afternoon. Here, come, let me show you. I'll sit in your place. I thought you were a man," as he took her hand and sidled to his place.

"I'm told our chauffeur waits for us without," our casket-maker repeated.

"Come, one and all," called the Commandant, seated at his place, and although still pale, recovered admirably from his hallucination, "a toast before you leave, and please, do take more of our repast. You've signed the report then and our business is dispatched?"

"Excellency . . . " began our priest, admonished by our Chairman to abide as he spoke for us.

"I'd have the rumor scotched," the Commandant interjected curtly, a manner of expression which had not heretofore shown itself.

"We will omit the nunnery," responded our Chairman.

"But, I'd have the rumor scotched once and for all," retorted the Commandant, as he stood at the table, flinging his glass of wine towards the door. "I say I'd have it scotched and will," as he fairly turned the table over and started towards the door.

"But for the matter of Rudin's appointment with the Lord Mayor, we've all but signed, Excellency," answered our Chairman, although weakly.

"I say he'll stay. My Yorick he will be, to play the fool for me. And, I'll have the rumor scotched. Who does this again? I mean to know the swine who brings the boot from twenty-nine!"

"Excuse the Commandant, dear friends," interceded his wife, as she tried to lead him from the room. "He has from childhood suffered a strange malady, which to take notice of will but turn it to an extreme. It is nothing. Pray you, finish your business that you may take your leave. Are you a man?" she asked of him.

"Man enough, as men go," he retorted. "Man enough where men are wanted. This world's not fit for living when boots can walk upended. It is the rumor that points the boot and I'd have it scotched, I say," he repeated, breathing heavily, his back turned to us, his head down.

"I bid you leave. Your car is waiting without. I'll take the report," his wife said, holding the door. "He is not well tonight. It was the day. He has a chill."

"I'd have it scotched, else they not leave," he demanded, still turned away, his voice breaking.

"Their leaving scotches it once and for all." Turning to us, "Please then, you will leave."

"Rudin then, for the nunnery?" rejoined our Chairman.

"So be it. I know he liked him well. He has little company of late. He is lonely."

"What is the rumor, madam, of which he speaks as though it touched his innermost sense?" asked our stonecarver.

"Poison from the pen of assassins. Words not fit to speak, yet spoken. Not fit to hear, yet heard; that the only way out of Auschwitz is as the boot points, through the chimney," she answered, taking the report. "Please, go now, while his thoughts are elsewhere."

I hesitated as the others walked on ahead, stopping at the door to look upon the Commandant, whose back was still turned. I was about to bid him farewell when he turned to look at me, a look I had not experienced before—lines not previously noticeable rending his face, the skin jaundiced, the lips trembling, aged now, his eyes piercing my own, then dropping, as he spoke hoarsely: "Thou Would Then Leave Me, Yorick?"

"Excellency ... " I tried to respond, as his wife bade me turn and leave, with a nod of her head.

My colleagues were in the car; our chauffeur warming the motor, which coughed in the moist, cold air. The car door closed. The gate opened.

You have to make another call? By all means. My address? The jewel? We're walking towards my flat. We'll see it as soon as we arrive, but a short walk from here. You'd like my address to telephone your fiancée where to meet us? Here is my card. Shall we say nine o'clock then? Excellent. I'll wait for you here, yes. No, I won't leave, I promise you. I would like you to see the jewel. Your fiancée as well. I look forward to meeting her anon. Yes, cher ami.

CHAPTER IX

I trust you found your fiancée at home and well. She is to meet you at nine? Very good. We have but a brief walk to my place. We could, if you choose, take a taxi. You seem ill. You haven't, I hope, become chilled. The night is cool, yes. You are perspiring heavily, cher ami. Please, let's take a refreshment in this air-conditioned pub. You would prefer to walk? As you wish, although I mean it sincerely that you should not overdo it. Sometimes we tax ourselves beyond our proper endurance, without realizing we are doing so.

The jewel? You know little of them and are afraid you might not appreciate its worth? That's modest of you, and most kind. You need not have any fear in that regard. This particular jewel does not require the lapidary's eye, although one might need to draw upon intuition, perhaps, as he would for the pendant. The pendant? It is that on which this jewel hangs. A simple one that one might purchase anywhere, not singular in design, yet, somehow it sets this particular jewel off.

Did we return to Warsaw that night? No. As

sometimes happens with automobiles, when least expected, the one which was taking us away seemed held as by some magnet within. Had our chauffeur had a better ear, he would have noticed that slight cough as the motor had been warming. We had to stop for carburetor trouble within a few dozen yards of the gate we had just driven through.

The region being swampy, the winter's cold of that kind which chilled to the marrow, I suggested a walk to my colleagues, that we might keep the blood in circulation, but they had already busied themselves with alacrity in holding a light here, a wrench there, to assist our driver, who cursed the Commandant's chauffeur with abandon, the latter having prevailed upon him, against his better judgment, to take a twirl about the compound. He insisted that he had sensed, from the first shifting of gears, that the car would never be the same again, and had it not been for the assistance and encouragement offered him by my colleagues, assuring him that they well understood from the trip without mishap coming down that he was without peer as a chauffeur, as they joined him in castigating the blundering driver on the compound, that one often ran into such ignorance in the countryside, he would have broken down completely. Fortified by our support, he bent himself to his task with admirable concentration, an occasional epithet hurled at the world an assurance of his professional skill.

Schooled from my apprenticeship with the adage that too many fingers spoil the soup, an appropriate motto for our craft, our instruments being delicate, often working with an eyepiece, I thought it best to walk about the countryside, keeping the car within easy hailing distance, an opportunity afforded to give some thought to all that had passed since leaving home, disturbed inwardly by the marked change in the countenance of the Commandant, debating whether I should approach the gate to see if he had retired yet, when my inner eye was drawn by a strange light in the distance, although outwardly I was not conscious that it had been.

You've had this experience, I'm sure. Perhaps we've had it today, wandering as we have from the west side docks along the Hudson and drawn, without our having realized it, to the southernmost tip of the island, from where your Harbor Lady was visible, when you took your leave to use the telephone, just as I've turned in the last while, without knowing I had turned, so that we are now but a few blocks from that flower vendor of whom I've spoken, not out of our way, I assure you; so my inner eye that night outside the gate caught that light without my being consciously aware of its presence. Had I looked in that direction with my outer eye, I very likely would have dismissed it as a peasant's cottage or a shepherd's lantern. And to-night, had I known we were walking in the direction of the flower vendor, I might have deliberately taken another turn, saying to myself that I had not really taken a turn away at all but that I was going towards my destination. Since, however, we are near, we might purchase a flower. My own is wilted, and yours, too, has seen its best moments. But then, they have, gracefully, as it were, adorning us, achieved old age with dignity.

The light? A railroad siding near another gate, which, having apparently approached it circui-tously under the guidance of the inner eye, seemed, as I became aware of it with the outer eye, geographically situated between myself and the car, although I couldn't be sure, and though it seemed (all is not as it seems) that I need but take a turn to my right and then hail the car, something told me that this might not be so, and my im-mediate inclination to take the turn and to shout with the lustiest voice I could muster, "Are you there?" or "Would it not be best if I helped?" or "Shall I see if I can find some hot coffee for us?" (ah, cher ami, some day a learned metaphysician will do a scholarly work on coffee, how not unlike cement, bonding man to man; there, look you there, across the street to that repair crew taking its accustomed break, that husky air-hammer operator returning with half a dozen coffees in paper cups for his comrades, two of them dark complected, and if I mistake me not, Negroes, they breaking bread together, about to exchange opinions upon life, their language of the earth, rough-hewn—who, pray, I ask, would trade these moments of comradeship over this most wonderful beverage?) as I say, inclined to call to my colleagues whether I might search behind one of the lanterns nearby for a coffee urn when my eye was caught by the whole scene before me (that moment when the outer and the inner eye strike the same plane simultaneously) the railroad siding, cast in a magnificent chiaroscuro, a switchman's lantern shaping a lazy arc as he signalled to the engineer, a warm light emanating from the windows of the depot, a dozen or more lanterns dotting the landscape at various distances from the center, casting more warmth, the outline of human figures behind and about the lanterns, a lazy hiss of steam and grinding of wheel on rails, as the great machine was coming to its halt—a scene worthy of Rembrandt's highest genius, one which I allowed to lave my mind's eye, unhurriedly now, assured by my reason that if lanterns were close by, coffee could not be far behind, sure that my colleagues would welcome a hot cup, thus, about to start towards the nearest lantern, not more than fifty yards away, in fact, to hail it, a lighthouse of a kind on this raw winter night, as I say, my sense of direction askew, when all of a sudden, a hundred searchlights turned on at once, blinding me as they blotted what had just been there, as though a modern painter, quite dissatisfied with what he saw, hurled a gallon of oil of vitriol upon the canvas to blot it out forever more.

As one comes from the womb naked, up-ended, slapped on the behind, startled by blinding light and a wild, shrieking sound of voices drumming delicate eardrums, echoing and re-echoing, I knew that nakedness again—blinded, a hard, wooden-like instrument slapping my behind, myself upended, if you please, my head down, my rear up, attempting to stand, but unable; on all fours now, not unlike my ancient counterpart in the riddle of the Sphinx. Whether the riddle has it that man as child is dizzy with nausea as he crawls, I cannot say, but my ears were ringing, for all the loud shrieking of the human voice, my eyes blinded from the glare of the searchlights, my stomach mashed against my other inwards. And, whether the riddle has it that we voyage by sea from childhood to manhood, I cannot say, yet it seemed that I was on an endless voyage, as though adrift as sole survivor in a small boat, approaching a rocky shore from which searchlights sirened a yellow glare, conscious of the boat's floundering, about to smash and splinter upon the rocks, then caught by a wave rising, rising higher and higher, unwilling to break, holding the boat aloft until I could nearly touch a promontory jutting out above the treacherous shore beneath, regaining momentary consciousness to look upon a bulldoglike countenance staring into my own, hearing myself utter the name, Javert, fainting away again as I pleaded that it was impossible to scale the cliff with my toes as it was made of steel fencing charged with current, that Jean Valjean had long since expired, his skull lying beside Alexander's at Eronisle.

But then, hearty laughter, even if guttural and husky, is laughter. I became aware for a second or two of a railroad depot as my head fell to the side, my periphery vision taking in at a sweep a long train of freight cars and a bustle of people searching for belongings and loud halloos shouted from car to car and the weeping which accompanies the arrival of kith and kin after long and uncomfortable travel through strange countryside, for I was at Warsaw and my mother and father were laughing as my uncle alighted of a Christmas eve and then there were tears mingled with laughter as they remembered how my paternal grandmother had spanked their bottoms for stealing strawberry preserves and how my own tears in the cafe as I spilled the coffee on my uncle's lap were dried by my mother as she picked me up and held me in her arms and carried me to the carriage which lurched to a start, and nestle as I would against her breast, the wind and snow were damp, swirling about my ears and neck, and there was the strange but warm murmur now of human speech that would not let me sleep and which I wanted to listen to because the land from which he came was so far away, Byelorussia, that there must be castles and kings and knights galore and all a child would dream upon. I could feel my mother nudge me and whisper to me to wake up that it was Christmas eve and I played the child and nuzzled my nose to her bosom, aching, tired, wanting to sleep some more in my childhood, listening, dozing, listening, waking, falling, dreaming, and a quiet, sad voice said, almost too soft to hear, "Will they spare the children, Maria?"

"I don't know, child," an older woman answered, hoarse from a wracking cough.

"You do, Maria. You've known Barca, the blind one. You're the only one she would talk to. Don't make me hate."

"Call it hate. As a child in Byelorussia, I watched them descend on us and cut my mother's belly open after three of them took her. They left eighteen of us in our village. A gypsy picked me up and carried me off to wander like a beast in the jungle, growing up on herbs and dried meat. . . . That was another century, a lifetime ago. . . . I am sorry, Leah. I tell you this to steel you. I have seen enough in the last months of the mocking torture of old men. My tongue glues. . . . Aye, and heard enough of the braying of asses as they deceived themselves and others, and known the hot shame of watching some buy their way through bar-

's steel, even to sell others. . . . Tfooh! Spit

barbarians for what they are, that have

eir Cross and twisted it into the figure of a

hildren. I say to spit on it and spit again

eathens that buried their Christ. . . . I'm

gpicker. Forgive me, child."

f Rachel, then? Call her from Barca."

be with Barca. Barca is blind. Can't

re? Did you see how they blud-

every side? He's more dead than

ildren?"

hild."

"

nd maybe yours. I am old,

hem the satisfaction of

hought of how my last

d. Don't think of it

One may try to take

nimal pleasure. Spit

their unholy terror

are nothing . . .

. That one you

, even with his

the way they

tears fall

the hard-

ourish that

and touch

spring and I

ss. I cry out,

on's strength,

ot know men

like a piece of

t behind. . . . I

d of love that is

"What then . . . of Rachel?"

"Before, when I was a child, they swooped
down like a sudden storm coming across the horizon from which you took flight the way the birds
do at the sudden appearance of the hawk, but
today there is something else come of two thousand years of hatred stored and hardened into a
kind of mold from which it cannot break loose,
like a pagan prayer to a new God of the street,
way they have. I have frightened you, more, forgive me. I carry something in my breast that is
twisting my soul into the soul of the damned,
crying out for the life of an oily rag, the ones they
have picked up in out of the way places which are
treated with more gentleness than they will be.
I cry out and weep inside and will not let tears
from my eyes because they would melt the hard-
ness that has come to my heart. I r

the joy of life, of creation, and I kiss your hand to only touch what you and David had. I knew it only from a distance. . . . Oh, how I've listened to men and women as I've been a scavenger in alleyways, listened to their whining after they had coupled in love, cursing each other with a miserliness of the soul, and I felt the curse of God on them for the evil as I sensed them yearning for a new God of hate in their image. I would then hold the rags tight in my hands to keep from crying out at the savagery and coldness of heart as it seeped into the street clefting men as the cold winds eddied, waiting for the black knight to roar across a continent, twisting the souls of nations, eclipsing the sun. . . . Had I been born a woman, I would have washed my lover's feet with my hair and kissed his hands with the tears of my love. . . . There was a touch of grace in your household. Your Rachel was born of love. . . ." Her voice broke. Leah was crying, trying to speak.

Maria asked hoarsely, "That one, has he said anything?"

"Sewers. The one word, when they threw him here," Leah replied.

"He speaks of the sewers of Warsaw. He is a partisan then. The uprising began yesterday and some have taken to the sewers. . . . Get him up. They're starting up ahead."

I was being shaken as a chorus of murmurs began near where I lay about the partisan who was with the uprising of the ghetto in Warsaw and one asking Maria to ask me whether I had known her son Phillip, another old woman whether I had known her son Abel alive, and I lay unable to move, unwilling or unable to open my eyes.

"Leave him be; give him air. They've beat him badly," shouted Maria to those who gathered around. "Rachel, bring Barca here to me and help your mother get him up. Pull him up, Leah. Take his arm. He carries a resemblance to your David. He can't move. Is he dead?"

"He's in pain, Mama. Look, his eyes are opening. He's trying to say something!"

Have you ever, cher ami, lost your power of speech? A fall down a cellar stairway, perhaps? Or a stray brick as you walked by a building under construction? I felt myself speak. I knew myself capable of speech, for I spoke and could hear myself but there was no sound. I said that my name was Rudin and that I was not a partisan. I could feel my lips move. I know my eyes reflected speech as they opened and looked into the eyes of the girl, Rachel, which, so luminous and understanding, spoke back to my own.

"He can't talk, Mama." She smiled. She was helping to hold me in a sitting position, my legs numb from the cold. I spoke again that I was not anyone they thought I might be and was looking for coffee and began peering about to see if the car was nearby only to find a hundred strangers peering back, anxious to learn of kith and kin, their faces a hundred mirrors finely cracked, bursting forth a hundred thousand visages reflecting pain, puzzlement or weariness of the soul. Shabbily dressed for the most part, they began speaking again, all at once, as though not believing that I had an aphasia but that I hadn't understood the language spoken, and each must have felt that his native tongue would be my own. There began shouts from the farther end of the crowd and guttural barks as there was a flurry of picking up meagre personal belongings. They were starting to move. The old woman named Maria reached down to help Rachel and her mother getting me to my feet, every bone in my body aching, an instant nausea seizing me again, causing me to heave bloody substance onto the snow. They pulled, all but carried me, my legs crumbling under my full weight.

"They mashed his stomach good," said Maria, wetting a rag in the snow to wash my face. "Did'st thou know a David Armoc, who was a partisan, husband to Leah who holds you?" I shook my head No, responded to no avail that I had not been in the sewers at Warsaw but here, on that very day, that I was about to leave and would speak to one of those men carrying a Tommy gun. She shook her head at me with pity, one of her eyes half closed, as though to help her decipher the movement of my lips, the signs my face made. "They mashed him badly, poor fellow, when they knew what he'd done."

I turned with appealing eyes to Leah Armoc, who held my left arm, begging that she understand. I had not been able to see her before, having distinguished only Rachel on my right and Maria. This was the woman, then, against whose bosom I had lain as I dreamed myself in a boat crashing upon a rocky shore. How in the name of anything that remains holy upon this earth or in heaven did you come to be here? Who is it that ravages the beauty of life in this way? Beautiful, beautiful woman of hair woven of silk, of eyes that shine as the sun, of mouth whose lips are as red as the pomegranate, goddess-shaped in brow, what curse was given to man that you are made to suffer for? I have strength enough now to place myself at your feet. Oh, woman, you were worthy of an hundred partisans who could withstand the scorching flame of a thousand dragons! She looked at me not knowing any of what I said, her eyes sad, but without tears, and asked me if I had known her husband, David Armoc, said to be a leader of the partisans for these five years past, she not having seen him in this time, the last news when an urchin of the street had brought her word that he lived, but no more than that, her appeals to him to lead her to where the information came from, as the urchin shined her shoes, unheeded, he disappearing as though swallowed by the ground. David was lame in the right leg. No, no, I had never known such a man; I shook my head, the only sign that I had understood, knowing that all I felt then could not be conveyed.

Those guards, if I could but get to those guards and make them understand, I would get through to the Commandant, but I was being carried, pulled, without strength to break myself loose, knowing, as I looked to my right, that we were moving away from the compound in the direction of that area which had been seen only from a distance that morning, over which chimneys hovered so solemnly.

Suddenly the column stopped, orders being issued from in front and behind and I gathered strength enough to stand alone that I might use my arms to reach into my pockets to find some means of identification. This was the first feel I had had of my clothing, my outer coat torn down the side, my trousers wet through, all that I had had in my pockets gone. I felt I would find speech as I stood before the guards and lurched towards them waving with my arms and hands, telling them I was with a Commission here, only on a walk from my car, which was leaving for Warsaw, as they burst into uncontrollable laughter, one of the huskier ones taking me by what was left of the collar of my coat.

"There's a fine clown for you," shouted one.

"A Mark Anthony without a tongue," laughed the other.

The laughter stopped, one of their SS superiors standing closeby, shouting at them to leave me alone, directing them a stern stare for their surliness. I felt someone at hand whom I thought I could trust and started towards him, his glare turning upon me as icily: "We'll have no trouble here. Get back where you belong." I shouted with my arms, his glare becoming ominous, his face flushed, "I told you to get back, you swine," taking his revolver from his holster. "You're here for work and there'll be no more of this insubordination tolerated," as I felt Leah's hand pulling at my arm. The officer's eyes left my face, looking at her, as he placed his revolver back in his holster and walked to those who had been laughing, speaking to them in an undertone as he nodded in our direction, after which he walked to another part of the column.

"You have no gun and you'd assault them?" said Maria, as I blanched white. "There'll be a time when you may take one with you."

The old woman, Barca, blind, holding herself to Maria with one arm, her other holding a cane, began to chant;

> The feet were weary, up they trod,
> Digging through the heavy sod,
> The shovels broke in earth of stone,
> While Rudin's jewel brightly shone.

"Who is this Rudin she talks about, and his jewel?" Leah asked Maria. I tried desperately to convey to them that I was Rudin as Maria answered;

"She speaks in riddles since she walked alone from Kiev. How she got across a thousand miles of tundra and forest, blind and halt, no one will ever know." I was nearly faint trying to make myself understood, shaking Barca to try to make her tell them who I was.

"It's a partisan, Barca, whipped out of his senses. Don't be frightened," Maria told her.

"The Lord spared Barca," Barca answered.

Barca, Barca, speak to them and tell them who I am and that I have the jewel.

"Give him this scarf, Rachel. He's cold. He shivers badly from lying in the snow." Leah gave Rachel her scarf. My teeth chattered uncontrollably. I had lost more than my speech now, standing mute, as Rachel touched my hand and tried to give me the scarf.

"Put it around his neck, Rachel. His collar's worn and torn." She smiled at me, almost imperceptibly, turned her eyes away.

"Take it, sir. I want to stay close to Mama. She is not well."

"Those with small children must come to the front. They must come now." A machine gun rat-a-tat-tatted to confirm it. Leah held Rachel close. A crying girl of twenty spoke truer truth that it was those with infants as she flung a child at my feet and began to sob as Maria took her by the hair and slapped her once, twice, thrice across the face.

"Filthy slut that'd abandon thy child," she shouted as she twisted her head from side to side, the girl tearing herself away falling, weeping. It wasn't hers but anothers; she had never married and had a child. Leah picked it up to hold it but Maria took the child from her and held it to her breast.

"Thou hast an angel of a child, Leah. Let me feel the suck of the little boy at my breast," as there were murmurs and cries and a guard stood by Maria saying;

"A pretty babe, but you have to get to the front while the water's hot enough for your showers. Hurry or you'll keep the others waiting. A pretty babe."

"I'll pluck thine eyes from thy head if thou dost look again upon the child," retorted Maria, without looking at him.

"Smelly hag. There'd not be water enough to wash you of your filth. Hurry on or I'll take him from you."

"Oh partisan," Maria turned to me. "Thou'lt allow Barca to hold thine arm. Thou'lt keep Leah and Rachel at thy side and be Armoc then?"

Maria, Maria, mother. I'll do as thee bid me do. I was once a man, I tried to say.

"Thou art a man, partisan, that has suffered much. Thine eyes speak to me. Kiss me, Rachel. I kiss thine eyes, Leah. Aye, child, thou suckest well and thou bringest the childless mother from out of the desert of alleyways. Farewell, Barca."

The young mother, untouched by any, looking at Leah's eyes, crying stood, and my feet were heavy, and my tongue now as I speak thick, as then, and Maria walked to her. "Come, child. Our babe has need of two mothers."

There was a swell and push of life and the wail of birth and more, as they stepped forth to obey.

Don't cry, Leah, don't cry. Oh Rachel, child, don't cry, but take and hold my arm. Oh Barca of Kiev, your blindness has not sealed your eyes from tears.

"They say that all of us must have a shower," said one of new arrivals behind.

"That they de-louse our clothes," another, "for Hitler's closet has need of them."

"That they issue us better ones then, mine no longer fit for wearing," said the first.

"That we'll be warmly fed afterwards," said the second. "Put the money that's in thy purse in thy shoe. Hurry, fool, while no one looks."

"It's said the drinking water should not be drunk without boiling," said the first.

"Since thou likest thy cup hot, 'twill serve thee to a tea. Come, let's help this lame couple behind. Thou'lt make a good crutch, for thou art sturdy with wit";

As a guard said to one on the side, "Give me your watch, old man. They'll steal it when you undress. Thieves abound within. I'll watch it for you. You're his wife? Let me keep your wedding ring. Afterwards, yes," winding the watch and backing away, listening to the seconds tick, smiling at them as there were murmurs behind;

"Why don't they give us a work card if we're here for work. Some went in the other gate."

"They said they start now; we'll start tomorrow."

"Aye, they mean to have us start in hell," retorted another, grim-visaged, eyes flashing.

"He talked about nothing but crematoria on the train," shrieked the other, lunging at him. "They ought to cut his gullet so he can't talk, the swine. He's too damn lazy to work."

"Where there's smoke there's fire! The devil's a saint beside these lying beasts," as Rachel tugged at my arm crying;

"Mama's frightened; she can't get up; she won't answer me!" The SS officer with holster had drawn near, his eyes on Leah who sat in the snow. He was barking guttural orders to move and left for the front.

Aye, Rachel, kneeling beside her. If I could but speak to her. Tell her I am Armoc. Your Mama's upset about the strawberry jam, as there was a shrill cry of "God, where art Thou!" The one behind with flashing eyes was leaping towards the guard with watch, followed by another, as wild dogs were loosed, the column surging, falling, breaking. Look at me, Rachel. We'll point our machine gun from the window when they come and nuzzle us with theirs. There, hear it go rat-a-tat-tat. Help me, Barca! She took her arm. The column quivered, wept, locked itself, fell ahead as hand touched hand and the watch stared shrieking tick-tock curses.

Hold my arm, Leah. I stumbled walking as she trembled from the cold. Rachel held her arm and Barca chanted in the silent snow.

Smile again, Leah. With your eyes alone, smile again, even as imperceptibly as you did a few moments ago.

Her words were almost inaudible. "They won't hurt Rachel? She works well. She is well brought up, good mannered, courteous. Show him how you can curtsy, Rachel."

"Mama, Mama, please," she began to cry again.

Leah, Leah, hold my arm tighter and know that you are beautiful and true and only Armoc has known you and will ever know and hold your head high for he was a partisan who believed in you and Rachel and living life, as there were cries from ahead and women being herded into a group that excluded men, young and older, but young enough, and the SS guard with holster pointed through to me and two Javerts lunged at Leah and smothered her sobs with hard hands as I tore at their faces and felt ice on my neck and snow in my face and a dizziness again that was nauseous.

You are Barca, old hag, not Leah, standing over me. Where is Leah, Barca? The nunnery is voluntary and no one need go to the nunnery who would not be a nun, for I had it so from his Excellency, the Commandant of Eronisle.

Rachel, you have aged. Who cut you across the face? Speak to me, child. Weep not for who was not your mother, for nuns do not have children and she has gone to the nunnery.

Hide your face, Rachel. Wrap this scarf about your head else they see that you are the picture of Leah and expel her from the nunnery for having a child. Let me kiss your tears away, child. Hold my arm.

"They will not cut her hair?" she bit her lips, trying not to cry. No, child, no. They'll not cut her hair. "She wore it long as my father loved it. Did you notice how beautiful it was? I sometimes helped her brush it as she told me of him whom I little remembered, of a carousel the best, that was not far from where we lived of a summer's night, and how he rode a roan stallion, my mother a bay horse, and I a shetland pony, until the music stopped. There, see there how the lights do play upon the sky as they did play that summer night and I stood by Maria as my mother and father waltzed and my father waltzed with me. My father was a school teacher who knew of many lands. Oh, look, how those tall brick towers do rise so high! They are, in this light, like the towers of Notre Dame which is in a picture on our wall. My father studied in Paris before I was born. There was a boy who loved me not far away when we could be friends so long ago who said he'd steal me away to be married at the Cathedral of Sacré Coeur in Paris, for he was Christian and insisted I would be his wife as one, and that from Montmartre one could see the whole of Paris and I said if he truly loved me he would be anything I chose him to be and he made us engaged with a pendant I wear about my neck and I asked my mother if papa would give me away at Montmartre and she said papa would give me to the one who loved me truly as a woman. Come, thou'll be my father, then. Do not frown, Father. I will visit thee, wherever thou art, for to be wedded is a joyous moment. I cannot help my trembling, Father. Hold my arm tighter; oh, be careful of my roses, and see, when he looks upon me there at the end of the aisle whether he truly loves me, for my veil will not let me look into his eyes now. Papa, thou tremblest so. Do not fear, for I shall love thee and mama always, close to my heart, and my love shall love thee, too."

"The wind is whistling through the poplars," chanted Barca.

"Thou art hard of hearing, Barca, for it is an organ that plays and thou my bridesmaid now," answered Rachel.

Aye, Barca. It's not the wind that whistles through the poplars. Do not speak more in riddles.

> The feet were weary, up they trod,
> Digging through the heavy sod,
> The shovels broke in earth of stone,
> While Rudin's jewel brightly shone.

Shut up, Barca. Shut up, I say. Hold my arm, child.

There were shouts and murmurs that he was there and someone was pulling me away from Rachel and I would not let them.

"That's him," it was the Chairman of the Commission.

No, no, I cried, speechless, throwing them away from me. I'll not leave her. Barca, tell them I am not Rudin.

"He's hurt. He can't talk!" It was the stone-carver.

"Are you sure that's him?" asked the guard.

No, no, I cried again, without utterance, I am Armoc and you will not take me away from Rachel. I hit the Chairman with all of my might across the face and pulled away from them to touch her again, to stay, to stay as what I was and no other, and fell to my knees before her to look up at her to ask her to understand and my heart had to reach my eyes so she could see as I tried to utter with my tongue and she looked with her own eyes and took my hand and kissed it and spoke with her eyes to mine and she didn't cry or smile and try to shame me but touched me gently with them as I'd never been touched with eyes before and let me ask her forgiveness with my own, her forgiveness and her love and she took the pendant from around her neck and placed it around my own and said, "Bless you, Father," and kissed me as Barca took her arm and they pulled me away.

Oh Rachel, child, Oh Rachel, love, that Thou did let me take Thine arm in my own and walk with Thee, that Thou did bless me, child, that Thou did bless a man that was less than a man, that Thou did suffer for me as the One to whom I had learned as a child to pray did suffer upon the Cross. He waited *then* for Thee, for Thou art His sister.

"Get him in the car!"

"How did he get way over here? Thank God we found him!"

"He's half frozen, wet through. He didn't mean to hit you."

"What was that guard saying to the driver about an uprising in Warsaw?"

"Hurry! The driver wants to get to the crossing before this train that's going out with a hundred cars on it. There's another train coming in; I can hear it."

"He's trying to talk! Rudin! Rudin! He's crying! That's a good sign!"

Forgive me if I made the sign of the Cross in public.

That's the flower stand, I believe, across the way. What's the matter? I know you've caught a chill. Can I help you? Are you sure? Please, do let me get you a fresh flower. This should be his place. Had I known in Paris who he was when I saw him feeding and training pigeons to home, I'd have given him the pendant. What's this, an old woman?

Madame, forgive me, but I was told this morning that there was a man, lame in one leg, who sold flowers in this block. This was his stand, you say? Was his name Armoc? David Armoc? What's that? What's that? Dead, three days now? But ... Buried in Potter's field! He had no family living! No ... no, I'm all right. Yes, yes, we would like a flower. Two, if you please. A red rose and a white, if we may. Bless you, too, and keep the change. No, I really didn't know him. I wish so, too, but it wasn't until this morning that I learned of his exact whereabouts. Yes, thank you again.

Come, dear friend, it's only a few minutes before nine, my lodging but across the way. You stare at her. You're very pale. Please, do let me call a doctor. At least, then, let's step into this pharmacy and find a medicine for you. You are perspiring heavily and I fear your fiancée will be overwrought. They may, by chance, dispense that ancient remedy used by the Shah of Persia. As you wish, then. Down this street.

The other members of the Commission? None are living. Our priest suffered a heart attack before we reached Warsaw; the stonecarver found his way to the resistance and was hung on a lamppost in the square; our singer became deranged. . . .

This way. Across the street. Will you be able

to manage four flights up? I am sorry for the lack
of an elevator.

My wife? Died during a bombing raid. My
daughter? They didn't release her.

The outer door is open. You'd prefer that I
walk ahead? I must apologize, dear friend, about
the poor lighting. I've complained to the landlord
on behalf of myself and the other tenants. He said
that when the ceilings on rent are lifted, he'll
provide searchlights if we like. It seems the tenants,
for the most part, being refugees of one kind or
another, soon accustomed themselves to the dimly
lit hallways.

We can rest on this landing. The last is the
hardest. Please, I beg of you, do not apologize.
We've come a long distance today. I only hope that
your fiancée will not mind the walk up.

The second occupation? I was approached,
after I was dismissed from the hospital, by an
emissary, who was assistant to the sculptor design-
ing a copper statue several stories tall, so placed
that it might be seen from great distances, of the
emancipator, wearing the tunic of permanent war,
the jewel you are about to see, sought as the
ultimate adornment to the statue. Rumor had preceded the emissary that if I could not be prevailed

upon, it should be brought to the attention of the emancipator, himself; that all he needed do was to wiggle his little finger at me and I would come posthaste. Under the circumstances, I refused. As it was then said in some of the cafes of my native city—Black is black, and white is white, if you're read, then you're all right.

There we are. I'll light this lamp. I hope you will not mind my locking the door, a necessary precaution. Would you have something to warm you? Brandy? Excellent. That's my drink, too.

Shall I bring the jewel then? Or, shall we wait for your fiancée? Please, then, make yourself at home while I get it, just in the other room.

The light is right. Yes, its carrying case, pure white, is the same in which I had placed it when I sealed it in the fireplace wall.

Has the brandy helped? Good. I am relieved. You may open the case, if you like. Please. It opens quite easily. There!

I see that you are dazzled by it!

The pendant, yes, the one of which I spoke.

Did I exaggerate its worth?

Can you understand what I meant when I said that men had crossed the sands of time to possess it; that it would be the final adornment to man's ultimate desire to BE?

Its value? Even though a jeweler's merchant who designed crowns of the most fabulous and select jewels, I could not put a price upon it. I have not felt worthy of beholding it, let alone having had it thrust into my possession under the circumstances I related.

Yes, it is remarkably heart-shaped.

It is yours, sir.

You do not possess the means?

It would take a kingdom to pay for it?

It should be put on display for the world to see?

You don't believe it's of stone of the earth? You may be right. What's that? You see a flaw? And another? Surely, sir, you jest! Ah, those almost invisible nicks into the very heart of the heart. It is the light you stand in! You have an inexperienced eye, sir. My craft is ancient. I have not been sought in every capital of the world for nought. This is the most perfect jewel wrought, I assure you. Here! I place this famous diamond once owned by the Empress Catherine next to it. Ah! You see then, how the diamond pales beside it!

Forgive my anxiety. I thought for a moment this was a ruse, your speaking of flaws to belittle it, to put me off my guard.

I'm so glad you mention that, the pendant, how naturally it compliments the jewel.

I believe a car has stopped in front. Your fiancée, perhaps? I should have drawn this blind. You grow wan! An unusual car, I would say. Surely, your fiancée does not go about carrying a strait-jacket over his arm. And his colleague in trenchcoat and fedora hat, a future in-law, perhaps? Then that was your call this afternoon, called a second time this evening. That's why you kept asking for my address.

You need not apologize. . . . You say you couldn't believe . . . that perhaps. . . .

Do take another look at the jewel! Know now that you were the first to behold it since the ancient parted with it.

Don't unlock that door! Stand where you are! That tiny pistol which had once been kept in my Warsaw desk is in my pocket. I believe I mentioned that I'm an expert shot. You didn't presume that I'd show this jewel without an exit prepared? You'd like to tell them to go away, they're from immigration, that you had erred? You'd like to call your fiancée? It's a little late, cher ami. I've encountered thieves before who worked on a grand scale and with perfect aplomb. Don't touch that jewel! Please, do turn your back now and face the wall.

Please, be so kind when I tell you to close your eyes and count to fifty. Let them knock; the door is hewn of oak.

I, too, am sorry that it had to take such a turn. I do ask that you give my kindest regards to your fiancée, if you really have one as you say. You see, I believed you . . . liked you very much . . . and had come to feel more than gratitude for your forbearance, sympathy. . . .

I mean it most sincerely when I say that I hope the chill is not too severe.

There, I have my toothbrush packed.

Please, forgive me, under the circumstances, not asking you to turn that we might shake our hands and bid each other a comradely farewell. . . . I hope we will meet again. . . . Cher ami, farewell. You may begin counting *now*. . . .

A 1 I S   n⁻¹q⁻¹
· 2σ
A 2 I S ·
· 6 -13